MICHELLE'S MARRIAGE DEAL

The Talmadge Sisters, Book Two

BARBARA MCMAHON

Chapter One

Michelle Talmadge hesitated at the office door. She should have called. But after so many refusals and fruitless appointments that she hoped would pan out, and hadn't, she wanted a face-to-face confrontation instead of a phone call. Joshua O'Malley's reputations was one of reliability. The insurance company she worked for used him repeatedly. Of course she'd never met the man. She hoped hiring him for personal business didn't constitute a conflict of interest with work.

Opening the door, she stepped into a small waiting area. There was no one behind the desk. Glancing at her watch, she saw it was just shy of five o'clock. She'd left work early to see the man. Had his secretary also left early?

"Hello, is anyone here?" she called.

The door to her right snapped open and a tall man filled the space, surveying her from head to toe.

"Looking for someone?" he asked.

She nodded, amazed at his height—easily several inches over six feet. When her gaze traveled up, she noticed he was topped by hair as black as midnight, with eyes as blue as the Irish sea. His face looked as if it had been hewn from the

Irish cliffs themselves, all angles and planes. Not particularly handsome, but arresting.

Intriguing.

Fascinating.

Instantly, she wondered how he made a living as a private investigator. She couldn't envision Joshua O'Malley creeping around incognito spying on cheating spouses or eavesdropping on criminal planning. He was too conspicuous.

Not to mention a bit intimidating.

Maybe a telephone call would've been better.

But she was already here, too late for would-have-been.

"I'm interested in hiring a private investigator to find someone," she blurted out, already regretting she hadn't made an appointment first.

He lifted a dark eyebrow. Glancing around the office, he frowned. "Where's Joyce?"

"Who?"

"My secretary cum office manager."

Scowling, he strode to the desk, snatched up a paper and read it quickly.

"Well, blast it all. She quit. She threatened it, but I didn't think she meant it."

Running his left hand through his hair, he left it messed and falling across his forehead.

Michelle tightened her grip on her purse to keep from giving in to the surprising urge to step closer and brush it back into place.

Had she lost her mind? She hadn't come here to indulge

in some sort of instant, unexpected attraction to a stranger. She needed a private investigator and he was the last one on her list.

She'd shied away from contacting him at first—because of his association with the insurance company she worked for. She didn't think there would be a conflict of interest, but wasn't sure.

After being refused by a half-dozen other agencies in New Orleans, she'd run out of names. Private investigators were supposed to be discreet. If he took her case, she'd rely on his keeping quiet as to the nature of her request. And it didn't involve any kind of connection with her company. Not that she held much influence with the large firm.

"There was no one here when I came in," she offered.

"I had a secretary. She stormed out a couple of hours ago. So it looks as if she wrote her note and walked out."

He looked to the door along the wall to the left which stood partially ajar. There was no one in that office, though following his glance, Michelle saw it was larger than the reception area, with two desks and a bunch of computer equipment.

"Guess they're both out," he said.

"Who?"

"The two operatives who work for me."

"Oh."

She tried to follow the conversation, but it wasn't getting to the point of her visit.

"Mr. O'Malley," she began. "I wish to retain your services to locate a missing person."

She'd been through the drill now six times. She knew it by heart.

He looked at her. "File a report with the cops? They usually handle missing persons situations for free."

She shook her head.

"Why not? "

"Well, I'm not sure he's precisely missing—I just don't know where he is."

He glanced at his watch. "I'd love to hear about a missing person who isn't missing, but I have to pick up my daughter at day care and I need to leave now. If I'm not there by six, she's history with them."

"I beg your pardon?"

"You don't want to know, lady. Come back in the morning—but not before nine. There'll be someone here then. I hope."

He turned back into his office.

Dumbfounded, Michelle remained where she stood. He wasn't even taking the time to listen to her. At least someone at each of the other agencies had listened.

One investigator had even agreed to help her. The proposed estimated expense had proved too prohibitive, however.

Would she find that the case here as well?

Joshua reappeared in only seconds, shrugging into a sports coat.

"Since neither of my operatives are here, I need to lock up," he said, opening the outside door and clearly waiting for her to leave.

"But I want to discuss hiring you," Michelle protested. It had taken a lot of planning to get here before five; she didn't intend to be dismissed so easily. Normally quiet and shy, she was growing more and more frustrated with how difficult it was to hire an investigator and that made her more determined than ever.

"Not today. I need to get to the preschool."

"Where is it? I'll ride along," she said recklessly. She couldn't take time off from work in the morning. She'd already taken a lot of time off to do her part in settling her grandmother's estate and getting the old antebellum home ready for sale.

Her boss had been understanding, but there was a limit.

Joshua looked at her in surprise. "I don't do business in my car."

Planting herself directly in front of him, Michelle stared up into his face. She was determined for him to at least listen to her.

Joshua looked at her, noticing for the first time how tall she was. She had to be five foot nine or ten. Most women made him feel like Gulliver in Lilliput Land. Not this one. She came to his chin and for one crazy moment he realized how easy it would be to kiss her—no contortions like he normally needed with the shorter women he dated.

When he dated.

Which hadn't been often in the last year.

Of course, if he'd met someone like this before, he might have been inclined to make more of an effort.

He shook his head. He didn't have time for such idle

speculation—he had a deadline to meet. Any interest in a new case came second to his little girl.

"What's your name?" he asked.

"Michelle Talmadge."

"Well, Michelle Talmadge, I have a kid to pick up. I can't be late. Not again. If you would call in the morning—"

"Maybe I should just try elsewhere," she said sharply.

Joshua took a deep breath. He needed the money. Things hadn't gone smoothly over the last year because of all the changes in his life with the arrival on his doorstep of his daughter Penny. He couldn't afford to turn away work.

But neither could he afford to be late again. The day care center had been extremely clear about that.

"Come on, then, Michelle Talmadge. Ever consider a career in private investigation? You're tenacious enough to qualify."

Michelle shook her head as she followed him down the hall and struggled to keep up with his long, impatient stride.

Joshua wasn't going to slow down. She could keep up or come another time.

When he stopped beside a beat-up old vehicle, she looked at it in surprise.

"This is your car?"

He smiled sardonically and opened his door. "Climb in, it's not locked. Who'd want to steal this wreck?"

Almost nodding in agreement, Michelle opened the passenger door, wincing at the loud screech it emitted. Gingerly she slid onto the seat. Surprisingly the inside of the car was immaculate. Ignoring the screech, she pulled the door shut with a strong thump.

He started the car, the engine turning over instantly, almost purring. Cool air was soon blasting from the vents.

"Sounds all right, anyway," she murmured, buckling her seat belt.

"Camouflage," he muttered. "Some of the places I go I don't want people to notice me. Who pays attention to a beat- up old car? But she has a top-notch engine."

She held on for dear life as he roared out to the parking garage as if to prove the prowess of the engine. Minutes later they were embroiled in New Orleans' rush hour traffic. They crawled along Magnolia Street, inching through four traffic signals before turning onto Canal Street.

Joshua wasn't the most patient of men. He beat a rough tattoo on the steering wheel, muttering under his breath and checking his watch at least once a minute. It might be faster to just get out and walk.

Michelle cleared her throat.

"About my hiring you," she said.

Joshua looked at her. "Okay, babe, let's hear the scoop."

Michelle winced.

Joshua slammed on brakes just missed crashing into the back of the car in front of them.

From the corner of his eye, he saw her wince again.

"I want you to locate my father," she said, staring out the windshield, as if afraid to take her eyes off the traffic. Maybe she wanted to brace herself for an impact.

"Name?"

"Sam Williams."

"Age?"

"I don't know exactly." She needed to explain to the man she didn't remember her father, that he'd left when she'd been just a toddler.

"Have a birth certificate?"

"For him?" she asked.

"No, for you."

"Yes. My sister has it with other family papers. I can get it."

"His age and place of birth should be on that. Unless your mother didn't name him as the father."

Michelle drew herself up, turning outraged eyes on the man.

"Of course my mother would have listed him as the father. They'd been married for years by the time I came along. They were very much in love."

Joshua snorted, and leaned on the horn as a motorcyclist tried to cut in. The man shot a look at Joshua and accelerated between two other cars, weaving his way through traffic.

"I should get one of those," Joshua muttered.

"Mr. O'Malley."

"Call me Josh, and I'll call you Michelle. So how long has your father been missing? And why don't you know how old he is?"

"He left Baton Rouge when I was two. That's twenty-three years ago."

He turned and looked at her. "Any reason for the delay in looking into this? I mean twenty-three years is a lot of time to sit on a missing person report. Didn't you notice he was missing during that time?"

"Actually, I'm not sure he considers himself missing. There were extenuating circumstances regarding his leaving. In fact, until just a few months ago, we thought he'd left voluntarily. Then we discovered he hadn't."

She twisted the straps of her purse and cringed when he pulled around a slow car, accelerated strongly then slammed on the brakes. They'd gained about fifty feet. Now traffic ahead of them was at a standstill.

"Blast it." Joshua pounded the stirring wheel again.

"Is there a problem?" Michelle asked, wondering if she'd made a tactical mistake in insisting she go with him. His driving skills were frightening. Maybe skills was too strong a word. She hoped she survived the experience long enough to reap any of the benefit hiring a private investigator might provide.

"I can't believe the traffic!"

"It's always bad at this time of day. I used to drive to work, but switched to walking and public transportation. It was easier."

And a lot less stressful, but she didn't think she should mention that at this particular moment.

When he looked at his watch again and frowned, she had to ask, "Are we under some kind of time deadline?"

"You got it in one, sister. If I don't get my kid out of the day care by six, she's history."

"You mentioned that before. I can't believe the facility would be so inflexible as to enforce such a ruling. Surely parents are a few minutes late from time to time."

He shot her a glance and grinned. "Probably. And they

were good about it the first dozen times. But it's chronic with us."

She cleared her throat. "Can't your wife pick up your child?"

"Nope, been dead for more than a year."

She opened her mouth to ask another question, but he raised his hand. "And before you start on another line of inquiry, I'll tell you so far I haven't been able to keep a housekeeper any longer than I can keep a secretary."

Michelle darted him a dark glance. Somehow she wasn't surprised to hear that. He about drove her crazy and she'd met him less than an hour ago.

"About my father," she said, changing the subject.

"Can't do it. Try the police," he said.

Disappointed, she considered her other options. At least he wasn't trying to charge enough money to pay off the national debt.

"I don't think the police will help. I just want someone to locate him."

"And do what?"

She blinked. She hadn't even thought that far ahead which she acknowledged. "Just locate him and tell me where he is. We'll take it from there."

"Who's we?" he asked.

"My sisters and me. We just found out a couple of months ago that he didn't abandon us as we were always told. Now we want to try to find him."

"After twenty-three years? That might not be so easy. What have you got for me to go on?"

"His name and if I get his age from my birth certificate, I can give you that. I do know he worked as an oil wildcatter twenty-three years ago. The company he worked for might still be around."

"Did you try asking them?"

She shook her head. "I don't know which company he worked for."

"Great."

He pulled off the jammed street onto a quiet one, winding his way through the modest neighborhood. He slammed to a stop by a colorful building which held the pre-school. A little girl dressed in denim overalls, white shirt, with a small baseball cap on her brown hair sat forlornly on the front steps. In her arms were papers and paintings and one ragged teddy bear. Beside her stood an older woman.

Michelle knew by the tight-lipped expression on the woman's face that Joshua had missed his deadline.

He checked his watch.

"Ten minutes late! You'd think they'd give me ten lousy minutes."

He thrust open the car door and strode over to the little girl.

Michelle watched as the child popped up from her step and raced to her father. Rolling down the window, letting out the lingering air-conditioned coolness and feeling the rush of sticky humid air, Michelle strained to hear what she was saying.

"I haff to take all my stuff," she said, offering her father the stack of papers, but retaining hold on the teddy bear.

The older woman walked down the sidewalk. "Mr. O'Malley. I'm sorry, but the center just can't allow this. We have been more then lenient with you. More so than any other parent in our group. But it is unfair to continue to expect us to bend the rules for you. I'm afraid you'll have to find other arrangements for Penny."

She handed him a large manila envelope.

"This contains her records. Good luck."

She gave Penny a quick hug and said something to the little girl. Michelle was relieved to find the woman could smile. At least she didn't leave the little girl thinking she was mad at her.

When she looked at Joshua, however, her heart skipped a beat. For such a large man, he looked curiously vulnerable. He squatted down near the little girl. Even so he still seemed huge. Reaching out an arm, he scooped her up and began walking slowly back to the car.

When Penny caught sight of Michelle, she ducked her head close to her father.

"Who's that?" she asked, studying Michelle warily.

"That's Michelle."

"Is she my new baby-sitter?"

"No, she's—" Joshua looked at her and shrugged. "She's just Michelle."

He made sure the little girl was buckled in the car seat in the backseat before he climbed behind the wheel.

Leaning back against the seat, he stared out the window.

"Let's go, Daddy, I'm hungry," Penny said.

"We have to drop Michelle back at the office so she can get her car," he said.

"I can find my own way back," she said.

It'd probably be safer than a return trip with Joshua's wild driving.

He'd made his position clear on her request, so there was really no need to continue this farce of a meeting. Tomorrow she'd have to go through the phone book again and see if there were any other agencies she could try. She was not giving up!

"We'll take you back." He started the engine.

Joshua hated having to fight his way through the traffic again to return to the office. But he still had to get to that side of town to go home. Maybe while there, he could find something for Penny to snack on. If he picked up some files to take home, he'd be that much farther ahead in the morning. With no baby-sitter and no day care for tomorrow, he'd be stuck at home with Penny while he looked for someone to take care of her.

"There are other day care facilities," Michelle said softly.

"I know, we've been in most of them."

He wondered if the first one would give them another chance. It had been almost a year.

"What you need is a housekeeper who'd be able to watch your daughter at home. Then you wouldn't have to worry about quitting time or meeting deadlines."

He looked at her. "What insight."

He shook his head, "Don't you think I've tried that route? What I need, Miss-Michelle-Talmadge-with-a-father-missing-for- twenty-three years is a wife. Someone who'd be there for Penny all the time, not just during the day.

Someone who could cook decent meals so we don't eat out so much at fast food places, and someone to keep clothes washed, hair trimmed. And someone who couldn't quit at the first sign of trouble." He glanced in the mirror, angled to see his daughter. She was talking to her teddy and seemed oblivious to the conversation in the front seat.

"Maybe you should consider that, then," Michelle said.

"Nope, tried that once—it didn't work."

It seemed unfair that the traffic on the return was much lighter. Joshua drove calmly. Michelle wasn't scared once. She was even a bit reluctant to say goodbye when he stopped near her car.

She shut the screeching door, and looked over the roof of the car when Joshua stood on his side.

"You'll be all right?" he asked.

"I may call again about your locating my father."

"First I need to locate someone to watch Penny. There's a lot you can do on your own. Try your birth certificate first. Then the company where he used to work if you can find out which one it was, or call around to the ones still in business. No sense wasting your money if you can discover the answer on your own."

"Thanks for the suggestions." She hesitated, but there was really nothing else. "Goodbye," Michelle said, wishing she didn't have to leave. There was something about the man that continued to intrigue her.

Joshua's words echoed that evening while Michelle prepared a light supper. Frustrated not to be able to hire anyone, she paced her small kitchen while she waited for the gumbo to heat. She was finding it much more difficult to hire a private investigator than she expected.

Either they weren't interested, like Joshua, or they wanted half of Fort Knox as an up-front retainer—with no guarantee they could come up with anything.

It'd been four months since her older sister, Caroline, had discovered that their father had not abandoned them as children as they had been told all their lives by their grandmother, Eugenia Talmadge. He had, instead, been forced away from his wife and family by Eugenia's machinations. She'd wanted a different alliance for her only daughter and had done her best to bring that about.

Michelle wondered what would have happened if her mother hadn't died so soon after her father had been threatened with a bogus murder charge and driven from the family home in Baton Rouge. Would her mother have found the strength and courage to search for her husband, or would she have given in to the demands of her strong-willed mother and turned to the man whose family fortune and historical lineage had been so important to Eugenia Talmadge?

It didn't matter. Her mother had died long ago—shortly after Michelle's younger sister's birth—leaving her three daughters to be raised by Eugenia.

Now her grandmother was dead and in dying had revealed the shameful situation to Michelle's sister Caroline. When her sister had discovered proof of her grandmother's interference, she'd been thrilled to learn that their father hadn't abandoned them.

Of course, Caroline's reconciliation with her husband, discovering she was pregnant, dealing with the estate and planning a new wedding had totally taken her focus off searching for their father.

Now living in the Garden District of New Orleans, renovating and restoring a huge old house she and Brandon had bought recently, and trying to get established in real estate in New Orleans, Caroline's life was totally full.

And happy.

Michelle didn't resent her sister's delight in her husband and the longed-for soon to arrive baby, but she was a bit envious.

And her younger sister Abby had her new job. She'd branched into trauma nursing, taking additional courses, working in the emergency room of one of New Orleans' busiest hospitals. She rarely spoke of the father who had left before she was born. And Michelle didn't bring him up often.

She ached to know what had happened to the man she didn't remember, but had missed all her life.

Giving the gumbo a stir, she vowed she wasn't going to stop now. She'd try Joshua's suggestions and see what she could find. And if needed, she'd approach him again. Or go back to the phone book and check out another agency. Maybe branch out to Baton Rouge or another city. She was determined to find someone willing to take on the assignment. Even if her father was dead, she wanted to know where Sam Williams had lived and what he'd done with his life.

Friday morning Joshua poured another cup of coffee and swallowed a mouthful. It burned all the way down. He didn't notice. He'd been on the phone for hours over the last two days, trying to find a day care with an opening for Penny.

It looked as if he'd run out of options.

His operatives had called a dozen times. One client had called, tracking him down at home, because of an error in the billing. And of course, he had no secretary to look into it. Joyce had probably invoiced the wrong amount, but he'd have to go to the office to get it straightened out.

And what would he do with Penny?

The doorbell rang.

"I'll get it!" Penny's voice called out as he heard her racing for the door.

"No!" he yelled.

She loved to open the door, but caution made sure he always knew who was there before letting her. Most of his cases were innocuous, paper tracing, but one never knew these days when some nut would seek him out for an imagined slight.

He looked through the peephole and then leaned his head against the door.

He didn't need this.

Opening it, he stared at Michelle Talmadge. Standing

squarely in the center of the doorway, he wanted to block any attempt at entry.

"Hello, Joshua," Michelle said brightly. "I've come to discuss the case."

"There is no case. I thought I told you a few days ago I couldn't help you."

"Please, I've taken time from work I can hardly afford." She grinned and shrugged. "I told them I was sick. I got the information you told me I could find. I forgot to tell you that we found someone not too long ago who actually knew our father. You can ask her questions we didn't think of."

"You can handle that yourself." He held Penny back when she tried to insert herself between him and the door jamb.

"At least listen to what I've found, please. Finding my father is really important to me."

"Yeah, well, so's keeping my kid important to me, and I don't think either one is going to happen." He turned and swept Penny up in his arm and made to shut the door.

"Wait." Michelle stepped inside, crowding against Josh and Penny. Her behavior was diametrically opposed to what she was used to doing, but she was getting desperate.

Joshua glared at her and then softened his expression as he looked at his daughter. "Why don't you get your bear and head back for your room? As soon as Michelle leaves, we'll have lunch."

"Okay." The little girl ducked her head and looked at Michelle with wide, curious eyes.

"She wears a baseball hat even in the house?" Michelle asked.

"Yes, do you have a problem with that?" His tone was belligerent.

Michelle smiled at Penny and shook her head.

When the little girl ran off down the hall, Joshua leaned against the hall wall and crossed his arms over his chest.

"I don't know how to make myself any clearer. I don't want to find your father. I've got other things of greater concern right now."

"What do you mean by your comment about keeping your daughter? Didn't you find a new day care center?"

He looked across the street, catching sight of his neighbor avidly staring in his direction. Her curiosity knew no bounds.

"You might as well come inside, no sense the whole world hearing."

And it would give him some small satisfaction to shut the door on Mrs. Turner's snooping.

Michelle looked around and saw Joshua's neighbor. She smiled politely and stepped aside so he could close the door.

Glancing around, she noted a child's clutter—books, crayons, toys, blocks. The TV sounded from the front room. Had she interrupted cartoons?

"This way," he said leading the way down the hall into the small kitchen. A table shoved against the wall held the remnants of their breakfast. Michelle said nothing, sitting gingerly on the chair he indicated.

"How did you find me?" he asked, sitting in another chair and tilting back on its rear legs.

"One of the operatives at your office said you were

working from home and sent me here when I said you were handling a case for me."

"Thought we cleared up the situation a couple of days ago," he said. "I'm not handling anything until I get Penny situated."

"I've contacted three more agencies—from listings in the phone book. They all said no, but one of them recommended you. Not that I needed the recommendation. You occasionally do some work for Acme Insurance Company—my employers. I figure that's about the best recommendation I can get. A search like this can't be that hard for someone as experienced as you. But I don't have a clue where to begin. I didn't even think of the birth certificate angle to obtain my father's age."

"Lady, I have a lot of other things on my mind right now. The last thing I need is to take on a new case."

"Business is so good you can refuse it?" she asked in surprise.

He slammed down the front legs of his chair, rose and crossed to the stove. "Want some coffee?"

"That'd be nice. Thank you."

"Business is on a downhill slide, but I can't concentrate on that without getting Penny settled first."

He filled two cups and brought them to the table. Placing one before Michelle, he took a sip of his and began to pace.

"If I don't find something soon, my goose is cooked."

Michelle licked her lips. "A live-in baby-sitter?"

"Tried that—had four. One quit right in the middle of the day."

At her look of surprise, he shrugged. "Penny's a bit spoiled. She can throw a terrific tantrum if it suits her."

"And day care is out?"

He nodded toward the phone. "I've been calling for two days straight. Either they're full, or they charge half a year's income, or they're ones we've already been thrown out of."

Michelle looked at him, trying to swallow the urge to giggle at the image. From what she'd seen of Penny, the little girl was delightful. Must be his propensity for tardiness.

"It's not funny. If I don't find something soon, I may have to let Penny go to her grandmother's."

"So there is someone to watch her."

"Yeah, she just happens to live in Atlanta."

"Oh."

"It's the last thing I want to do."

Michelle nodded in agreement. "Little girls need their fathers. I know. I didn't have mine."

He glared at her. "If there was another way, don't you think I'd leap at it? Fathers happen to want their little girls, too."

Stunned, Michelle tried to figure out if her father had felt the same over the years. Had he missed his daughters all these years as much as she'd missed him? Wouldn't he have done all he could to see them once they were grown? she wondered.

She could sympathize with Josh O'Malley's desire to

keep his daughter if only for his daughter's sake.

"Maybe you should really consider getting a wife," she suggested hesitantly.

"Totally out of the question. Absolutely and positively no! Good grief, I think I'd kill myself first."

Michelle blinked. "So why don't you tell me how you really feel about the suggestion?"

Chapter Two

He stopped pacing and leaned a shoulder against the wall, sipping from his cup.

"Maybe you can guess, my first venture into marriage wasn't the greatest thing since sliced bread."

For a moment, Michelle didn't register what he'd said. She'd just had the most incredible idea. It was the most outlandish scheme she'd ever thought of. And Abby was usually the one in the family to come up with outrageous ideas. Still, it was a measure of how desperately she wanted to locate her father and how completely frustrated she felt with no progress in all the months she'd been trying.

"Maybe not a real wife," she said slowly, thinking aloud. "What about a business one?"

Turning so she could face him, she warmed to her idea.

"Someone, say, who worked where there was childcare provided for employees. Who'd be glad to help you out in your time of need in exchange for your services in her time of need."

His eyes narrowed. "Don't tell me, let me guess. The paragon just happens to be you."

She nodded. "Yes, but wait before you say no. I know

it's totally off the wall. But think about it for a minute. You have something I need—expertise in tracing lost persons. I have something you can't seem to get——day care for your daughter."

"So you take her into that child-care at your work? Where does the marriage bit come in?"

"That's the sticky part—only children, or stepchildren, of employees can use the day care center. But there's no question of it being too crowded or even costing anything. It's a perk of the company. And it'd eliminate any worry of anyone kicking Penny out if I'm a few minutes late picking her up. It's set up to accommodate different hours with all the parents. What do you think?"

"I think you're nuts. Absolutely certifiable."

But he narrowed his eyes and gazed at her closely. Michelle could almost see the wheels turning in his mind.

She regarded him gravely. "Maybe. But I really, really want this. I'm not sure I can explain it fully. All my life I've been curious about my father. Until a short time ago, my sisters and I thought he'd abandoned us when we were babies. But we recently found out differently."

"Sounds like abandonment to me—if he never got in touch with you in twenty-some years. What makes you think he wants to be found? Or wants to establish any kind of contact?"

"Oh, I don't need to contact him necessarily. At least I think I don't. But I do want to know what happened to him. See if he needs anything. I make a good salary at the insurance company. My older sister, Caroline, has a huge house now in the Garden District, with extra bedrooms and all. Between us, we could do something for him if he needs help."

"He could be dead."

She nodded.

"I almost wish that were so. It'd make it easier to know he couldn't have returned than to know he just turned his back on us and kept going," she said slowly. "But it doesn't matter, I want to know what happened to him. I really need to know or go crazy."

"So for the price of finding out, you're willing to marry a stranger?"

She hesitated a moment, then nodded. "Temporarily. And only as a business marriage that would suit us both. Though to my work, we'd have to pretend it's real."

Her heart raced. She'd never proposed anything so crazy before in her life. Yet the thought of that precious little girl going hundreds of miles away from her daddy really hit Michelle hard. She'd have given anything to have had her father be part of her life when she was growing up. For a moment, she remembered that young girl who had so desperately wanted a daddy. The thought of Penny losing hers was too much.

"What I think is that you are crazy," he said.

Michelle rose and crossed to the sink.

"Actually, maybe you're right. I can see all the advantages on your side and little on mine. Would you expect me to wash all these dishes?" The sink was piled high.

He stepped beside her and tugged her away. "I don't need another wife."

She smiled up at him. "Yes, you do. I could make dinner each night, make sure Penny went to bed on time. And free you from all domestic worries so you could find my father. It's a perfect business arrangement."

He stared at her for a long time—as if assessing if she were real. Finally he nodded. "If that's all it is."

She scanned him from head to toe, then met his gaze.

"Afraid I want you for some nefarious purpose?"

He laughed at that and shook his head. Walking to his chair he dropped down on it, putting his empty cup on the table. "Not with a face like mine. How long do you propose we stay married?"

"I don't know, until we no longer have to be I guess."

She hadn't thought that far ahead. In fact, she hadn't given the idea more than a split second consideration. If she did any thinking at all, she'd probably realize this was one of the dumbest ideas in the world. Marriage wasn't something to jump into and then out of.

Yet, if it enabled her to locate her father, it'd be worth it.

And she liked children. She and Penny would probably get along great. And she'd help keep a little girl with her daddy.

"So you'd be Penny's step mama for a while?"

"I wouldn't do anything to worm my way into her affections. I wouldn't want her to get attached and then miss me when we get the marriage annulled. But for the time being she'd be able to go to the day care at the company."

And Josh could search for her father.

"Annulled." He held her gaze. "That's what you're planning?"

Unexpected heat rose in her cheeks as a totally different image sprang to mind. That of Josh kissing her, holding her. She shook her head to clear the vision. Whoa, she was looking for a way to enable him to take her case, nothing else.

"I'm proposing a marriage of convenience, not the real thing," she said firmly, wondering if that would end up being enough.

"And in exchange I locate your father."

She nodded again.

"Let me think about it."

"There's one more thing," she said slowly, suddenly feeling awkward. Why now after already broaching the ridiculous subject she didn't know. But the awkwardness grew steadily. Clearing her throat, she tilted her chin. "I'd have to live here in New Orleans so we'd have to pretend to my family that it's real."

"Why?"

"My sister Caroline's pregnant. She miscarried her first pregnancy and we don't want anything upsetting her this time. If we pretend to be married for real, she won't have anything to worry about. We don't have to tell her about our deal. Time enough after the baby's born."

"Let me get this straight—in exchange for searching for your father, we get married, pretend to the world we're madly in love, and you'll take Penny to day care, live here and cook?"

Michelle nodded slowly. Saying it aloud made it sound totally preposterous. Glancing around the kitchen, she smiled brightly. "I'm a great cook."

"Do you realize most of the time I'm in the office during the day and home every night like any businessman, but there are occasions when I need to go somewhere on business or handle a surveillance, or monitor some particular activity which means I won't be home that night? Are you willing to watch Penny under those circumstances?"

"Of course. I'll be living here."

She didn't want to tell him she normally didn't have much to do in the evenings. That'd lead to all sorts of questions she didn't care to answer.

He studied her for a long moment, then rose.

"I'll think about your offer."

Feeling let down, Michelle nodded. She was sure once she had a chance to think about what she'd just suggested, she'd change her mind. But for a few minutes it seemed so perfect.

How long could it take him to find her father? Even a few months pretending to be married wouldn't be a hardship. Just until Caroline had her baby. She'd help him out with Penny.

"I'll leave you my number," she said.

"That won't be necessary. If I can't find you here in New Orleans, how do you ever expect me to find your father?" he drawled.

Michelle felt like an idiot as she headed out to the Garden District to visit her sister. Since she wasn't working today, she might as well make the most of her day off. But she continued to dwell on her meeting with Josh. What had possessed her to offer a marriage of convenience? The man probably suspected she had ulterior motives and wanted something else.

And she didn't want to involve her sisters. Brandon and Caroline had enough with their baby coming and renovating their new house. From something Caroline had said, Michelle wasn't sure her older sister felt strongly about actually finding their father. She seemed satisfied for now to learn that he had not abandoned them as children. Of course with all the recent changes in her life, she didn't have time to go searching.

Caroline had held the belief for years that she'd been the reason for their father's desertion. Discovering the truth had ended that lie and gone a long way into making Caroline more trusting around men—and her estranged husband Brandon in particular. They had reconciled and were now expecting. With her move, new job, new home, it was no wonder she didn't have time to search for a missing person. Michelle wouldn't expect her to.

But she could. She'd lived in her apartment for four years, no work needed there. She currently wasn't dating anyone. Work was steady and dependable.

Michelle and Abby had discussed trying to locate their father, but for the time being, her younger sister was too wrapped up in her new nursing course and her normal duties to have time to explore further.

That left it up to Michelle. She was the perfect one to go searching.

Wistfully she wondered if her father had missed her after he'd left. Whatever he'd done since then didn't matter to her. She just wanted to *know*.

Caroline wasn't home. Michelle was disappointed. With nothing else pressing, she headed for the nearest mall. She'd indulge herself by shopping this afternoon. And hope there was a message from Josh on her answering machine when she returned home.

Her phone rang as Michelle entered her apartment several hours later. She dumped her bags and pulled it from her purse. Had Josh decided?

No such luck. Caroline's face filled her screen.

"Hi Sis, how are you?" Caroline's serene voice came across the line.

"Hi, I'm doing fine. More importantly, how are you?" Michelle ignored the tinge of disappointment she felt that it wasn't Josh. "Hold a minute. I just got in and have groceries to put away."

"No rush, I just called to chat. Brandon's working late tonight. Call me when you have a minute."

"So we're both eating alone? I'll call you while I eat, so we can have dinner together," Michelle suggested.

While a good cook, she rarely prepared a full meal for herself—saving that effort for when she had friends over.

Tonight she heated some soup, toasted French bread and cut up fresh fruit for a salad. Then she called Caroline.

She didn't know what Josh would decide, but just in case, she'd better lay the groundwork with her family. Caroline would worry just as much with an unexpected wedding as she would knowing the circumstances behind this one.

"I haven't seen you in ages," Caroline said, once the preliminaries were out of the way.

"I've been busy," Michelle said, taking a deep breath. "Actually, there's this guy—"

Silence greeted her announcement. She frowned. Was it so shocking that she could attract a man?

"Really?" Caroline asked, a hint of excitement in her voice.

"Really. His name is Josh."

"Where did you meet him? When? Does he work at where you do? How serious are you?" Caroline asked.

Michelle laughed at the barrage of questions. "Whoa, slow down. Let's see. I met him at the office." No need to mention which office. "He works for the company sometimes. He does investigations for insurance claims." She held her breath. Would Caroline suspect?

"Tell all," her sister demanded.

"Well, we've been out a few times." All right, once, to the day care center to pick up Penny. Not exactly a date, but Caroline never needed to know that. And would coffee at his house also count?

"It just sort of took off from there."

"What did?"

"Our feelings for each other," Michelle said recklessly.

"My God, you're seriously interested in the man?"

"Definitely!" Seriously interested in having him find their father!

"I can't believe it! Tell me everything. Does Abby know?"

"Uh, not yet. She's been busy, you've been busy and I've certainly been busy." Looking for a private investigator.

"When can I meet him?"

"There's nothing definite between us yet. I'm not exactly sure how he feels." Except about marriage, she thought with a touch of amusement. He'd made himself perfectly clear on that subject.

"Tell me all about him."

In describing Josh, Michelle realized she apparently noticed a lot more about the man than she'd thought. Not only his physical characteristics, but some of his mannerisms, like that impatient energy that had to find an outlet in pounding a steering wheel or pacing a small kitchen.

She made no mention of Penny. If it didn't work out, if she had to find another way to locate her father, she didn't want Caroline or Abby to know more than the bare bones.

"Bring Josh to dinner on Sunday," Caroline ordered.

"I'll have to check and let you know." Michelle panicked. She hadn't expected that. What if Josh said no to her crazy proposal? What if he refused to go along with a charade to fool her sisters?

"I've got to go now, Caroline. Give my love to Brandon."

She hung up feeling wrung out. Setting the stage was difficult. If Josh agreed to her scheme, could she carry off the deception?

It depended on how badly she wanted to find her father—and protect her sister.

Caroline had been protecting her all her life. She owed it to her to make sure she kept her from worrying.

The doctor had assured Caroline she'd be fine this

pregnancy, but Michelle remembered how devastated her older sister had been after her miscarriage and had no intention of being a cause of unnecessary worry or concern.

She was already in bed and leafing through a magazine when the phone rang again.

Her heart skipped a beat when she recognized Josh's deep voice.

Without any preliminaries he went to the heart of the matter.

"You've got yourself a deal, Michelle."

The enormity of what she'd done almost overwhelmed her.

"Thank you," she said primly.

"Want to discuss particulars now or in the morning?" he asked.

"In the morning." Panic threatened. She needed some time to assimilate the fact she would soon be marrying a stranger, pretending an emotion she didn't feel, and be half responsible for a little girl who by her daddy's own admission was spoiled and sometimes threw tantrums. Was she crazy?

"We'll pick you up at nine and head for Dunking Delights. Penny loves donuts."

"Fine."

Hanging up, Michelle stared blankly at the opposite wall. Her heart pounded, her throat felt dry. Could she go through with this? Or had she made the biggest mistake of her life?

She shook off her doubts. How hard could it be to

pretend for a few hours here and there in front of her sisters that she was a happily married woman? The rest of the time she and Josh would go their separate ways.

Saturday morning she dressed in yellow shorts and a white loose cotton top. The weather forecaster predicted high temperatures and higher humidity. She wished she lived near the water where there was a chance of a breeze. Instead, her apartment was hemmed in by others, keeping any wafts of cool air to a minimum.

Ready long before the appointed time, Michelle paced in front of her window, stopping suddenly when she realized she was copying Josh.

There was nothing to be nervous about—it was a straightforward business deal. They each brought something that the other needed. And in no time, they'd be able to obtain an annulment and go their separate ways.

But the churning in her stomach didn't abate. Nervously, she wiped damp palms on her shorts and began pacing again.

The doorbell startled her. It rang and rang.

Opening the door, she saw Penny still pressing the button.

"That's enough, Penny," Josh said reaching for her little hand, his eyes on Michelle.

"I like it," the little girl said, dancing away from her father's reach and spying a doorbell by a nearby door. She raced down the hall and began pressing it.

"Penny! No!" Josh called, quickly following after her to snatch her up just as an elderly woman opened her door and peered out.

"Yes?" she said.

"Sorry, Mrs. Hatterly. Penny's fascinated by doorbells," Michelle said, as she joined Josh and took his arm, tugging toward her open door. "We didn't mean to bother you."

The older woman nodded vaguely and shut her door.

"It's wrong to ring doorbells if you aren't going to visit the people who live there," Michelle said to Penny.

"She doesn't know that," Josh said.

"She'll never learn any younger." Eyeing him suspiciously, she frowned. "Something else we need to discuss, I see."

"What?"

"Discipline, manners."

He took a sharp breath through his nose.

"I'd say we have more than that to discuss. Ready?"

Michelle reached inside for her purse then shut her door. "Ready as I'll ever be."

Feeling much like Alice in Wonderland where nothing was quite normal, she headed for the stairs.

Settled at the table for four at the Dunking Delight, Michelle watched Josh allow Penny to order two huge jelly-filled donuts. Michelle had eaten her own breakfast a couple of hours ago and settled for a latte.

Once seated, Penny began to eat, one foot kicking the table leg.

Josh bit into a light glazed doughnut.

"Penny, stop kicking the table, please," Michelle said, patiently.

"Don't gots to," she mumbled, licking jelly from her fingers, her foot swinging again.

"Yes, you do," she said, her tone brooking no refusal.

Josh looked up at her in surprise.

"She's just a kid," he said defensively.

"Which is the best age to learn proper behavior in public."

Penny looked from one to the other, her eyes wide. But she stopped kicking the table leg.

"She's four years old," Josh said.

"And as I mentioned after the doorbells, we obviously need to discuss discipline. Children need rules and boundaries. How do you expect her to learn proper behavior if you don't guide her?"

"She's fine. We don't go out much."

"Oh, that's a great answer. What if you need to go out, do you want a child no one else wants around?"

Penny's eyes filled with tears.

"Daddy?" she said. "I don't like her."

"I'm beginning to side with you, kid," he said glaring at Michelle. "You're starting to sound like Penny's grandmother."

Michelle raised an eyebrow. "My sympathies are with the woman."

"Well they shouldn't be. She ruined her daughter and would ruin Penny if I gave her the chance. Penny's just a kid. Time enough to learn things later."

"When?" Michelle asked.

"I don't know, later."

She shook her head, took a sip of latte and sighed.

It wouldn't work. She had no need to worry about how

she'd relate to the father, if she couldn't even relate to the child.

Looking around the restaurant, she noticed other children with their parents. Happy islands in the impersonal public place. A woman laughed at something her son said, while her husband beamed indulgently.

A twinge of envy struck. Michelle would love to be part of a happy family like that. To have a husband who loved her and their children. Who would find time to spend with his family on inconsequential outings like this. A family to build memories with and to reassure their children they were loved.

"Penny, go play in the kiddie section," Josh said.

"I'm not done." She'd eaten most of one doughnut, Michelle noticed when she looked at her. Or at least decimated the doughnut. It was a toss-up how much was inside and how much smeared on her hands and face. Josh calmly wiped up as much of the jelly as he could, and sent her to the kiddie area blocked off in one corner of the yard of the restaurant.

Tossing the sticky napkins on the table he narrowed his gaze at her.

"Tell me what makes you such an expert on rearing kids. If my information is correct, you have never married, never had children, never even been exposed to children."

"What information?" she asked, diverted.

He looked guilty for half a second. "A cursory investigation."

"You had me investigated?" Dumbfounded, she could only stare at him.

"I didn't have you investigated, I did it myself. You're twenty-five years old, have an older sister named Caroline who is married to Brandon Madison. A younger sister named Abby, who's a nurse at St. Joseph's. You were valedictorian at your high school but for some reason elected not to proceed to college but instead got a job at Acme Insurance company where you've worked your way up to a supervisory position with lots of responsibility and a certain amount of prestige in the company. Impressive for one so young."

"Is that all?" she asked outraged he'd do such a thing.

Yet also intrigued he'd found out so much in only a day.

"No current boyfriend," he said slowly. "Of course it was only a quick and dirty look-see, but I don't find information about any boyfriends."

Heat flushed through her cheeks. Except for one boy in high school, he wouldn't find any serious ones over the years.

"Maybe I ought to hire an investigator to look into your background," she snapped.

"You're changing the subject. I'm asking about your experience with children."

"Discipline is the word you're looking for, Josh O'Malley. And it appears to be sadly lacking in Penny's life."

"You were raised by your grandmother—some starched-up society dame in Baton Rouge. You probably went to deportment class," he returned.

Michelle almost nodded, but it was none of his business. She was not advocating Penny be raised as strictly as she and her sisters had been. But there was a happy medium between her deportment lessons and Penny's free-for-all.

"At least I know how to behave in public," she said as he kept his gaze steadily on her.

"What?"

"Come on, Josh, use some common sense. Haven't you been in restaurants where an obnoxious child has ruined the pleasure of dining for you? Ever been at the movies where a rambunctious child talked, spilled his drink or kicked your seat back—ruining your enjoyment of the show?"

Slowly he nodded. "But Penny—"

"It has little to do with Penny and more to do with her father and his permitting her to behave that way," she interrupted.

Leaning back in his chair, he scowled at her.

"She's just a little girl," he said again.

"Get over it, Josh. She's tiny compared to you, but then most people will be, you're so tall. I'm not saying act harshly toward her, just show her the right way to behave."

"Her mother and I didn't get on at the end. Hell, we didn't get on from the day we returned from the honeymoon, I think. We divorced right after Penny was born and Sylvia got custody. So I didn't see much of her until last year when her mother died and she came to live with me. And with her mother gone, I'm trying to make it up to her."

"She's your daughter. She needs to know you love her."

For a moment, Michelle's anger spiked so strongly that she wish her father had felt the same, had defied her grandmother, stayed to fight and been there for her while she was growing up.

"And part of that caring is raising her to know how to

behave. You'll do more harm if she doesn't have any acceptable manners. No one expects a four year old to behave like an adult, but expectations are that children gradually learn and get better as they grow."

"I won't tolerate interference with how I raise my daughter," he said.

Michelle nodded. "I've had time to think this over and it was a dumb idea in the first place. Even dumber if you think I'm going to live in your house and ignore her behavior. Let me pay for breakfast and we'll call it quits," she said.

He looked at her in surprise.

For a moment Josh felt a touch of panic. He hadn't been sure he wanted to agree with Michelle's crazy plan, but it did buy him time to find a more permanent arrangement for Penny. If he agreed to the scheme, he'd have help with Penny— maybe until she was enrolled in school. By then, he could see about after-school day care. He'd figure it out. This marriage bought him some time. And enabled him to keep his daughter.

But to do that, he needed Michelle to follow through with her suggestion. Not fold when he laid down a condition.

He looked over at Penny. She was playing alone on one of the crawl toys the kiddie center provided. She had difficulty relating to the other children at the day care centers and the preschools he'd tried. She was wild and undisciplined. But she was so little and so adorable. And he loved her more than life itself.

He couldn't let her grandmother raise her. He'd miss her

too much. He wanted to be there for her, see her grow up, hear about the exciting things she learned in school, even mop up tears when some punk boy hurt her as a teenager.

But if he didn't take advantage of Michelle's offer, he was at his wits' end on what to do.

"For the duration of our mock marriage, she'll be your daughter. I don't abide spanking, but I'll listen to your suggestions," he said heavily.

Surprised by Michelle's startled look, he wondered what she thought of him. Would she have even considered talking with him if she didn't need his skill to locate her father?

For the first time he really looked at Michelle. She was pretty in a quiet, unassuming way. Her deep auburn hair was pulled back, then curled around and beneath the bow she wore. Her bright blue eyes were guileless, always meeting his directly, hiding nothing. She was quiet and reserved in a manner as unlike his ex-wife Sylvia as anyone could be. Maybe it wouldn't be all bad working together for a few months.

"I can't devote full-time investigation to your father," he said suddenly, wanting to be up-front with her. "This arrangement will help me out, but I also need cases that will pay hard cash. I'll do the best I can to expedite the search."

"I understand."

"Of course I'm always juggling a dozen or more cases at a time, so what's one more? And I have a couple of operatives who are skilled in different areas, I'll also assign them to some of the background work."

"Someone needs to talk with Edith Strong."

"Who's Edith Strong?"

"She knew my parents. She was a contemporary of my grandmother's and may know some specific information about my father. She's the one, besides grandmother, who finally told us the truth about my father's leaving."

"Then interviewing her will be a high number on the list of things to do," Josh said.

"So, we're on?" she asked.

"I'm in if you are. Penny turns five in July and starts kindergarten in the fall. If we stay together until then, I should be able to locate your father and find suitable after school care for her."

She cleared her throat, toying with the napkin on the table. "Actually, it would have to be a bit longer— until my sister Caroline has her baby in November."

He nodded. "Okay."

"When do you want to get married?"

"Tomorrow," he said dryly.

"What?"

Smiling at her astonishment, Josh felt a huge weight disappear. She was still hanging in there. For the first time he was glad he hadn't found a boyfriend in the background who'd object to her bizarre suggestion.

Though he didn't understand the other men in Louisiana. Michelle might be quiet, but she was pretty. Why hadn't she been married long before—to some guy who still believed in love and all that stuff?

"I want to get Penny into the day care as soon as possible. You set the date," he said.

"You're right. You need her taken care of. Get her established in a normal routine. I don't mind getting married soon."

She bit her lip, as a sudden thought hit.

"What?" he asked. Would he always be able to read this woman who would soon be his wife? Unlikely, he'd never been able to understand Sylvia. But Michelle seemed to express everything right up front.

"I'd say we could elope, but my sisters would never forgive me. Especially Caroline. She and her husband eloped a few years ago and then renewed their vows earlier this month with a full church ceremony. She puts a lot of stock in tradition."

"Sorry, I draw the line there. I've been through that once. This is not going to turn into a multimedia circus event to keep your sisters from suspecting anything."

"Of course not. I wouldn't want to spend the money on something so frivolous unless this was a real marriage. But we have to do something or they'll suspect something is up. And then Caroline would worry and try to protect me when she needs to concentrate on delivering a healthy baby."

"We'll do what your sister did—elope and tell them we plan a formal ceremony later."

Michelle shook her head. "No. Caroline would fret and I can't have that."

"Are you expecting that our entire marriage will be dictated by your sister whom I've never even met?"

"You can meet her tomorrow. She's invited us to her place for dinner."

"When was this?"

"Last night, before you called. I didn't know if you'd say yes or no to this crazy arrangement, but I thought I should set the stage—just in case."

"Just how did you set this stage?" he asked suspiciously.

Michelle told him and by the time she'd finished, Penny appeared at her dad's side.

"I want to go," she said, eyeing Michelle cautiously.

"Michelle and I haven't finished talking," Josh said. He watched Penny closely in case she threw a tantrum at not getting her way.

"Isn't there a park nearby? I thought we passed one just a few blocks away," Michelle suggested. "That'd be fun, wouldn't it Penny? You can play on the swings while your Daddy and I finish our discussion."

The little girl nodded warily.

Settled on a park bench a short time later, Michelle waited while Josh went over the rules of where Penny could go and where she couldn't.

"Ground rules," Josh said, joining her on the bench.

"Right. I know we'll still need to watch her. What else did you want to discuss?"

"You'll move into my place to be there to take care of Penny. It's not big, but we have a third bedroom. Do you want to move your own bed in, or use the Hide- A-Bed that's already there?"

"I'd prefer my own bed," she said. Suddenly the knowledge she'd have to give up her apartment hit her. "My apartment."

"What about it?"

"I don't want to lose it."

"Sublet it."

Biting her lip in indecision, Michelle didn't know if that would work. "How long do you think this will take?"

"I would expect to find as much as I can in the next few weeks, maybe a couple of months. We may get lucky and it will only take a couple weeks. But I've agreed to stay your husband until your sister has her baby. Or, if I don't find your father by then, we'll just extend the arrangement until I do locate him."

Five months? He looked away at the thought. They were committed to sharing a house, meals, events as a family. She'd even share temporarily in raising his daughter.

He hadn't considered all the ins and outs. And especially how Penny would react.

He appreciated Michelle's planning to help but not ingratiate herself with Penny, keeping in mind they'd separate within a few months. He hoped his daughter didn't become attached.

He couldn't believe he'd agreed. His employees and friends would have a field day teasing him after his tirade on marriage and the scathing comments he made about Sylvia.

This was a business proposition. Nothing more! He wished he could let everyone know that. But he'd given his word for the sake of Caroline. He would honor that commitment.

"I'll sublet. I guess I can move my furniture into your place. Or store what there's no room for," Michelle said.

"I have a garage we can use. It's half full of stuff anyway, I don't use it for the car."

"I'll do the cooking and the laundry. Can you do the vacuuming and picking up?"

He nodded. "I'm used to doing it all, so to have you do the cooking is worth your weight in gold. Especially if you're as good as you say."

"Oh, I am."

When she smiled at her cocky answer, Josh felt a second of awareness that he hadn't felt in a long time. He knew Michelle was pretty, but not for him. Not again. He quickly turned away, searching the playing children until he located Penny.

"I can contribute equally to the family coffers," she said into the silence.

He glared at her. "I can afford to support my own family."

"True, but this is different. Since I work, I can contribute. I insist on paying my own expenses."

"You're doing a lot by providing the day care."

"Do you know what some of your competition was going to charge me had I been able to afford it?"

"No."

Gazing into her eyes, Josh realized he didn't know about the competition and didn't care. Suddenly he wanted to know more about Michelle Talmadge—more than what he'd found for the preliminary report he'd compiled. The surface information was easily obtained. But he was curious about what lay beneath. She puzzled him and he loved solving puzzles.

Not that he'd let his interest carry him away. He'd learned his lesson when married to Sylvia. No more entanglements with women. Actually, Michelle was doing him a favor, by providing a solid barrier for the next few months against other females who thought they could entice him.

She looked at him expectantly.

"What?" he said.

"I asked about your getting a new secretary."

"I haven't found one yet. Why?"

"Maybe I could help out in the evenings if you still need help. Organization is my thing."

"I noticed that from your personnel records. You've received a lot of commendations."

"And just how did you get into them?"

"I told your supervisor I was doing a high-level security investigation and she showed them to me."

"All of them?"

"The glowing commendations, the praises for the innovative techniques that saved time and money and made reporting easier, and the hefty raises you've received over the years. You should be proud of yourself doing so well in a predominantly man's field."

"One day I'm going to return the favor," she warned darkly.

He laughed. "Don't be like all the other women I know who think being a private investigator is exciting and romantic. Most of it's a lot of researching records and files.

Or sitting in a car waiting for someone to do something stupid."

"It's not dangerous, is it?"

"Not the field I specialize in. You're thinking of TV shows or the movies. Those private detectives are practically supermen."

She nodded. "My offer still stands."

Josh studied her for a moment. "Thanks. I might need the help if I can't find someone soon. Back to this marriage, are you sure we can't elope?"

"I'm positive. But it doesn't have to be an elaborate wedding. In fact the more low-key we keep it the better. But I will want my sisters there and you must have one or two friends who should come for appearance sake."

"I have a couple I'll ask."

She was right, the fewer who knew the real truth surrounding their marriage, the fewer explanations they'd have to come up with. More of the world was romantic than cynical. Any story they told would feed that romanticism—unless they told the truth.

Michelle glanced at Penny. "I wonder if we could do everything by next Saturday?" she asked.

"Depending upon what you mean by everything. A simple ceremony before a judge shouldn't be that complicated. You're the one who'd want the fancy dress and all."

"I can buy a dress in a day. So does next Saturday suit you?"

"Yeah." He stretched his long legs out and leaned back in the bench, slipping his fingers in the tops of his pockets. "I can't believe I'm doing this," he said watching Penny play.

"If you'd rather not—"

"No, it'll work. I'll see to it."

Michelle nodded. "Me, too."

Chapter Three

Michelle stared at Caroline's house, butterflies kick boxing in her stomach. Nervous, she tried deep breathing, then stopped, afraid she'd hyperventilate. She could do this, she repeated, wondering if she was fooling herself.

Though lying had never been an easy skill of hers, surely she could convince her sister, and Brandon, that she and the man beside her were madly in love and couldn't wait to get married.

The man beside her.

She looked at him. Meeting his gaze, she was startled by the amusement in his eyes.

"I don't think this is funny," she said.

"You look as if you're going to an execution. Relax. I thought you liked your sister."

"I do. I love her. But what if she suspects this isn't a normal marriage? If I can't convince her, she'll worry and that's definitely not something I want happening."

Josh shrugged. "I've worked undercover before. You imagine the part, then step in. Didn't you ever do plays or something when in school?"

"No." She'd been too shy.

"Well, it's easy. Just go along with the role you've created."

She nodded and took another deep breath.

"Of course, you understand props. We need props to make it work."

Swinging her gaze at him again she shook her head. "What props?"

"This for one."

Josh leaned over and kissed her soundly on her surprised mouth.

It wasn't just a light brushing of lips but a full-blown kiss. Michelle's eyes widened, then slowly drifted closed as her senses kicked in and became embroiled with the sensations that suddenly exploded inside.

Her heart raced, the butterflies forgotten as heat swept through her like the hottest Louisiana sunshine. When he pulled back, she slowly opened her eyes and stared at him in bemusement.

"Better," he said, running his hands through her hair, mussing it up.

"Stop, what are you doing?"

"Setting the stage. You want your sister to believe we're in love, right?"

Michelle thought she did, but with the blood pounding through her veins and the echo of thunder in her ears from his kiss, she was having trouble thinking at all!

"At least wait until there's an audience," Michelle said, opening the screeching passenger door.

Josh got out and swung around the front of his car to catch up with her quick walk up the walkway. He hadn't expected anything from that kiss—just to tease her into a better frame of mind. Now, he wondered what had hit him. And would it happen again if he kissed her a second time? He was glad Penny was staying with a neighbor. He wasn't ready for her to see the two of them kissing.

Michelle rang the doorbell as Josh joined her on the wide wooden porch. Glancing around she looked everywhere but at him.

"Chill out, babe. It was only a kiss."

At that her gaze snapped up at him. "Don't call me babe!"

Josh smiled and leaned closer—so close Michelle could breathe his scent, that tangy spicy aftershave and the unique scent that was Josh's alone—male and magical. She swallowed hard and tried to ignore the fluttering of her heart. This was make-believe—nothing more.

"Think of it as a term of affection."

"It brings to mind tight skirts and slinky women."

"Ah, now that's an interesting image." His gaze ran down the length of her and Michelle was hard pressed not to turn around and storm back to the car. Maybe coming tonight had been a mistake. He wasn't touching her, yet she felt every inch come alive. She wanted to push him away, rail against the unfairness of the situation—he was deliberately provoking her and she had no way to retaliate. Not now. Just you wait, she thought. Some place, some time when you least expect it—

"Maybe we should explore this a bit more—word association. If babe brings slinky women to mind, what do you think about when I say hot as honey?"

Michelle drew herself up and tightened her lips. "Will you behave? We're here to make sure Caroline and Brandon believe we're madly in love. Provoking me isn't the way to prove that!"

"Prove what?" Caroline opened the door and looked from her sister's angry gaze to the amusement dancing in the eyes of the man standing next to her. Slowly she smiled.

"You must be Josh," she said, holding out a hand.

"And you're Caroline." He shook her hand and ushered Michelle into the cool house, his hand warm on her lower back.

Michelle forced a smile, kissing Caroline's cheek. "Yes, this is Josh."

"Annoyed, are you?" Caroline asked, her own smile wide and amused.

"He's enough to drive a saint to do something crazy."

"And I never even *pretended* to be a *saint,"* Josh said.

"Come and meet my husband," Caroline said, walking down the wide hallway toward a large room in the back. Windows covered one wall, bringing the lovely garden into the room.

Michelle wished she'd come up with some other way to have Caroline be assured about what she was doing. But now that they were here, she'd have to make the most of it.

Brandon turned to her after greeting Josh and kissed her lightly on the cheek. His eyes missed nothing, from her heightened color to the mussed hair Josh had tousled. He sought Caroline and they shared a look.

Michelle refused to be annoyed. At least she was over her stage fright.

Until Josh placed his arm across her shoulders and walked with her to the sofa. Sitting much too close, he settled right beside her. His leg pressed against hers, his arm encircled her shoulders. She felt surrounded, crowded. Aware.

Toying with her low pony tail, Josh calmly answered Brandon's questions and Caroline's gentle probing. But Michelle couldn't concentrate. Her entire being was caught up in the emotions that raced through her. His casual attention touched something deep inside.

Surprised, she found she liked it.

And that scared her. She wasn't a woman to be attracted to some man just because he made a play for her. And in this case, Josh was almost ignoring her talking with Caroline and Brandon. Yet she couldn't shake the awareness that grew with each second.

"I made shrimp Creole," Caroline said looking at Michelle. "Want to help me with the last bit?"

Michelle nodded and jumped up. Suddenly realizing that would mean leaving Josh alone with Brandon, she hesitated. "Will you be all right here?" she asked, turning her back on Brandon and narrowing her gaze at Josh.

He nodded. "I think I can defend myself until you return."

She had to hope he would.

Once in the huge old-fashioned kitchen, Caroline peeked around the door one last time then rounded on her sister.

"He's amazing. And obviously crazy about you— he can't keep his hands off. Where did you find him?"

"I told you, he does investigations for my company."

Trying to remember her own role, she smiled and wondered if it looked dreamy or just spaced out. "He's wonderful, isn't he? You do like him, right?"

"So far." Caroline narrowed her eyes. "Just how involved are you?"

Michelle took a deep breath and prayed this would work. "Involved enough to invite you to our wedding!"

"Wow!" Caroline hugged her. "I can't believe it. Does Abby know?"

"Not yet. I wanted to make sure you met him and liked him. But I'll call her when I get home."

"Nope, we'll call now. She'd never forgive us if we left her out. Brandon!" Caroline went to the door. "Do we have any champagne? We're celebrating! Did you know Josh and Michelle are engaged?"

She whirled around without waiting for an answer and hurried across the kitchen. "So when will you get married? Christmas is so lovely. But June is a wonderful month, too."

"Actually, we thought about June as well—but this year, not next. Are you free next Saturday?"

Caroline stopped and turned to look at her sister. *"Next Saturday?"*

Michelle wished she'd waited to tell that bit of news. Caroline looked stunned.

Maybe the entire idea was bad to begin with.

No maybe about that actually.   But they were committed.

"Are you all right? Should you sit down?" Michelle hoped the shock wouldn't be too much for her sister.

"I'm fine. Stunned, but fine. Why the rush?"

Michelle shrugged. "I don't want a big wedding. So why not get married right away? I mean we talked it over and both want to, so why not just do it and then...move...in...together."

It sounded weak.

Or was it her guilty conscience talking? She wasn't sure.

Wishing Caroline would at least look happy again, she wondered what else she could add to convince her sister this was a good idea.

Brandon walked into the kitchen, followed by Josh.

"I guess you told her, huh?" Josh said.

Michelle nodded as Brandon crossed to the refrigerator and rummaged in it for a tall bottle of champagne.

"How do you think she's taking it?" she whispered, watching her sister.

Josh leaned over and kissed her, then held her chin with his hand. "I'd say your sister is going to need a bit of time to get used to this." Looking directly at Caroline, he raised an eyebrow. "Right?"

"To say the least. Congratulations. But next Saturday?"

"We don't want to wait," he said.

"Is there any reason for the rush? I mean, another week or two. Or month or two. Just so you both can be sure."

Brandon opened the bottle with a loud pop. Quickly filling three glasses, he handed one to Josh and to Michelle. "Sorry, darling, you'll have to have water. But you can still join in the toast."

"Brandon, they're talking about getting married this next Saturday—six days from now."

He slipped his arm around her waist and drew her close. "You can't remember back six years? We didn't want to wait, either."

"I guess." Caroline looked doubtful as she gazed at Michelle and then Josh as if trying to wrap her head around the idea of her sister getting married in less than a week.

Michelle knew she should say something to convince her she was happy and this is what she wanted, but she was tongue tied. It was all moving too fast. Everything seemed to be spinning out of control—not the least of which was the way her senses went haywire the minute Josh touched her.

He clinked his glass against hers and sipped the sparkling beverage. She drank a gulp and her eyes watered with the sudden burst of bubbles. At her exclamation, Josh brushed his lips across hers, winking at her look of astonishment.

With wobbly knees, Michelle leaned against him, wishing she could get him away from her sister long enough to deliver a blistering sermon on why he had to stop kissing her!

"If you two are sure, who are we to second-guess you?" Caroline said. "Let's call Abby."

Michelle smiled and nodded. Relief hit her. Caroline suspected nothing, and wouldn't worry.

Glancing at Josh, she swallowed. Maybe Caroline wouldn't worry, but suddenly Michelle wondered what she thought she was doing—marrying a total stranger who affected her as no one else ever had.

"That went well, don't you think?" Josh asked three hours later when he opened the passenger door for Michelle. Brandon and Caroline remained on the porch, illuminated by the overhead light. Waving once more, Michelle climbed in and winced when the door gave its usual loud screech.

"Wouldn't oil fix that problem?" she asked when Josh slid in behind the wheel a moment later.

"What problem?"

"The door and the awful noise it makes!" she said, knowing she was looking for something to vent her frustration on. She refused to give voice to the uncertainties that plagued her. The door might as well take the brunt of her emotions.

Josh started the car and smoothly pulled out into the street. "I'll see about oiling it tomorrow," he said.

Annoyed he'd given in so easily, she frowned and stared out through the windshield.

"Anything else?" he asked in a bland voice.

She flicked him a look. "Like what?"

"I don't know, that's why I'm asking. I can't read minds. But I can read body language and you are uptight about something. What?"

Michelle opened her mouth to tell him, then snapped it shut. She wasn't sure she even knew what had her so upset. It had to do with the kisses he'd given her, and the feelings that churned inside her and the uncertainty about what she'd proposed.

"You've been this way since we arrived at your sister's," Josh added.

"Well, you didn't help matters."

"What?"

"Fiddling with my hair, putting your arm on my shoulders, kissing me." She smoothed the material of her skirt, tracing the material with a fingertip.

"And here I thought we handled the romantic setting well. That's what people do who are in love. I thought we were trying to convince your sister and her husband."

Michelle nodded. She was being silly, she knew. But she'd never expected the wash of awareness and attraction that flooded through her just being near Josh. She couldn't afford to let herself fall for the man. They had a business agreement. And she had to stick to her part of the bargain if she wanted him to stick to his.

And she did.

Wistfully she gazed out the window. She'd so wanted to find out about her father. Wouldn't her old-family conscious grandmother have a fit to know Michelle hadn't considered the Talmadges the be-all and end-all of families? She yearned to know about her Williams side.

"Michelle?"

"What?" She blinked and looked at Josh.

"I lost you for a moment. We were talking about acting like lovers at your sister's."

Acting like lovers. The image that sprang to mind was not easily banished.

Michelle stared at Josh in the sporadic light from other vehicles as he drove. He was not handsome in a traditional sense, but strong and masculine and totally fascinating.

What would it be like to be lovers?

She had never fallen in love, never lasting forever love.

What would it be like with Josh? He made her feel different—on the edge of something thrilling. He gave her a heightened awareness of the potential between a man and a woman. Her blood still raced through her veins and it'd been hours since his kiss.

She cleared her throat. "I guess you did what you thought was necessary to project that image."

"Would you have had us behave as mere acquaintances?"

"No. It was just so unexpected."

"Why? I told you I'd act the part. I'm good at undercover activities."

She couldn't tell him the unexpected aspect had to do with her own reaction to his kisses, not his throwing himself into the role.

"I'll remember that."

"Are we going to spend a lot of time with Caroline and Brandon? Or your sister Abby?" he asked.

"Probably not, why?"

"Just wondered how often we'd have to play this game."

Of course, without the audience they had to convince, there'd be no reason for kisses and caresses.

"Well, there will be some occasions," she hedged.

While she didn't think she could remain impervious to

his touch, neither was she willing to entirely forego the pleasure in the future—if she could come up with a reason to indulge.

Good grief, was she losing her mind?

"We will see them next Saturday at the wedding. They'll expect us to want to be alone for a while. So you won't have to draw on your powers of subterfuge."

"I wasn't complaining."

He reached out and captured one of her hands, linking his fingers through hers and resting them on one muscular thigh. Michelle caught her breath, aware of the tingle of awareness that shimmered through her from their linked hands.

"I liked it. Didn't you?"

She mumbled something, once again caught up in the whirlwind of sensations that seemed to short-circuit her brain.

"I liked your sister and her husband. They almost make a man believe in marriage."

"What?"

"My own experience wasn't so hot, but watching them is like peering into a private love fest. He obviously adores her and she hangs on his every word with matching adoration in her every glance. Haven't they been married for a while?"

"Yes and no," Michelle said slowly.

Josh glanced at her. "You're good at that—ambiguous answers. They either have or they haven't. Right?"

"They've been married over six years, but only lived together for a few months at the beginning, then were separated for five years. They got back together this spring."

"The reason for the separation?"

"The miscarriage started it, but my grandmother perpetuated it," Michelle said shortly.

"Ah, the same grandmother who drove your father away. She sounds like a real charmer. Sorry I missed getting to meet her."

"I suspect you'd have given her a run for her money."

"If we find your father, that will be the best revenge," he said with another friendly squeeze on her hand.

"So after Saturday, you won't have to pretend to be in love for a while," Michelle said, more to remind herself than to tell Josh. "Do you want me to get Penny a dress for the wedding?"

"Good luck. The kid doesn't wear dresses."

"Why not?"

"Shorts are good for play. The only time I tried to get her into a dress she threw a hissy fit, so I haven't tried since. She, uh, might not want to come without her hat."

"Does she sleep with it?"

"No, but she wears it all the time when she's not asleep."

"Why?"

"I don't know—she likes it."

"Well, prevail upon her to forego it for one day. I would think a little girl would love to dress up for a special outing."

Josh shook his head. "I don't know, Michelle. Maybe we should just let her wear shorts."

"I could come over Wednesday night and take her shopping to see if we could find something for her."

He was silent for a moment, then shrugged. "Fine with me. I'll take us out to dinner and then we'll see how it goes."

He pulled in to the curb and stopped in front of Michelle's apartment.

"No need to get out. I'll be fine," she said brightly.

"No problem." He stopped the car and got out, going around to open her door.

Michelle didn't wince at the screech this time. Was she beginning to get used to it?

Silently they took the elevator to her floor and walked down the quiet hall. Stopping by her door, she fished out her keys.

"Thanks for coming with me," she said, fumbling with the lock.

Josh's hand covered hers, guiding in the key and turning it.

"I enjoyed meeting Caroline and Brandon. Are you all right?"

Michelle nodded and smiled brightly. "Sure."

"You seem nervous. You did pretty good with the pretense, except you seemed startled every time I touched you."

"Well—"

"Maybe all you need is practice."

"What?"

"You know the old saying, practice makes perfect."

With that, he covered her mouth with his.

Michelle was breathing hard when he lifted his head and gazed down at her, his expression giving nothing away.

"Better. See, practice is the key."

"Good night, Josh," she said and almost flew through the door, closing it in his face.

Her knees felt wobbly and her heart raced. She still felt the wonderful imprint of his lips against hers. Instead of acting like a scared schoolgirl, she should have pretended to have a certain level of sophistication and kissed him right back.

Leaning against the door, she sighed. She did need more practice if she was to pull this off and not give rise to speculation.

Just how much would be enough?

Chapter Four

Michelle was surprised at the anticipation that built as Wednesday afternoon progressed. Josh had called that morning to say he'd pick her up at six. Never a clock watcher, Michelle seemed to check the time every ten minutes. Giving in to the excitement, she left work early and hurried home to change into something more suitable for shopping than her business suit and heels.

Josh had reiterated the invitation to dinner, and she wondered where they would go? Another fast food place for Penny, or a family restaurant?

Wearing a loose, gauzy sun dress and sandals, Michelle was ready when the doorbell rang. From the incessant sound, she knew Penny was the one pushing the button.

"Hi," Michelle opened the door and caught her breath. She hadn't seen Josh since Sunday.

Why did looking into his eyes cause her heart to jump and then pound?

Forcing her gaze down, she smiled at Penny.

"Hi, Penny, ready to go shopping?"

The little girl leaned against her father's leg and shook her head. Her shorts and shirt were neat and clean. The cap sat squarely on her head.

"Don't gots to."

"Don't have to," Michelle corrected gently. "But it would be a lot of fun. We'll buy you a pretty dress to wear on Saturday, and maybe shiny shoes."

Penny watched her warily and shook her head, clutching her teddy bear tightly. Her baseball cap shadowed her face, but Michelle caught the stubborn pout.

Josh picked her up and looked at Michelle. She saw the family resemblance, and the family solidarity. Hadn't they worked things out yet?

"Ready to eat?" Josh asked.

"I am." Michelle slipped her keys into her purse and slung it over one shoulder. Pulling the door shut, she tested it to make sure it was locked. "Where are we going?"

"There's a nice place near the Quarter that's fine for kids. That'll put us close to some of the department stores on Canal Street."

The place Josh chose was perfect for families. And it was early enough to be uncrowded.

Michelle made small talk until they ordered. The restaurant provided crayons and a black-and-white menu for children with a scene for them to color. Penny began industriously coloring in the background with bright blue.

"Any place special you shop for her clothes?" Michelle asked.

"No. I've only had her for a year. Some of the clothes her mother bought still fit. And we haven't had any occasion to buy fancy dresses before this. Besides, she hates to shop."

Michelle looked at the little girl, then her father. "Does she or is it you?"

Josh glanced at Penny. "I'm not so thrilled with it. Do you know how tiny the buttons are on kids' clothes?"

Hiding a smile, Michelle nodded. "Maybe it'll be easier with the two of us. I promise to fasten all the tiny buttons."

"Most of the time shorts and a shirt are enough."

"But not at a wedding," Michelle said firmly.

"Speaking of which, did you make the arrangements?" Josh asked. They had agreed she would handle that aspect, and let her siblings know when and where.

She nodded. "At noon, at the courthouse. Judge Thompson. It'll only take a few minutes and then we can all go to lunch. Abby and Caroline insist I have to stay with Caroline Friday night and have Brandon give me away."

Josh looked at her. "You're not wearing some fancy white dress with a veil and big bouquet of roses, are you?"

"I could," she said, teasing.

He closed his eyes. "I thought this was going to be a small wedding, in and out, so to speak."

Laughing softly, Michelle reached out and patted his arm, snatching her hand back when she realized what she'd done. "It will be. I have a nice white suit and a skimpy hat with a tiny veil. Maybe you'll give me a corsage or something."

"Yeah, that sounds great. Lunch and then we're done, right?"

She nodded, feeling a pang with the thought of the ceremony. Once upon a time she'd thought she'd find a wonderful man to marry and raise a family with. There was still that possibility, but this would be her first wedding. And for her sisters' sake, she had to make it seem as real as possible.

"You're not expecting a honeymoon, are you?" he asked.

"Of course not."

He looked relieved. Michelle wondered what he really thought about this crazy plan.

"In fact, Josh, except for the few times you and I have to be with my family, you can continue to live your life just as you always do. I don't plan to interfere."

"For the last year, my life's been pretty much tied up with Penny."

"Before that?"

"Before that, Sylvia had custody and wasn't really generous with allowing me time to see her. Something always seemed to come up at the last moment."

"That must have been hard."

He nodded.

Michelle waited for him to say more, but he didn't. She glanced at Penny. The picture on the menu was almost fully colored. She hoped the meal arrived soon. She was running out of things to say.

"Look, Daddy, I'm coloring good." Penny held up the picture. Scribbles ran over all the lines. Michelle didn't think she remembered seeing a green elephant before.

"Wonderful, Penny. I like your picture." Josh's tone was sincere and full of love.

Watching them, Michelle's heart melted. He was so obviously proud of his daughter it warmed her from head to toe. How much she'd missed in her own life by not having her parents while she grew up. She never remembered her grandmother being so proud of anything she'd attempted.

"Show Michelle."

"Don't gots to," Penny said slapping the picture down on the table and frowning at Michelle.

"I can see it from here. It's pretty," she said, refusing to be hurt by the child's actions.

"Turn the sheet over, baby, and draw a new picture on the back," Josh suggested with an apologetic glance at Michelle.

Once Penny was again engrossed in coloring, Michelle shrugged. "It's all right if she doesn't warm up right away. From what you've said, she's had a lot of different people in her life over the last year. She's probably protecting herself by not getting too friendly until she knows if I'll be around for a while or not. Wise on her part. We both know I won't be around for the long term."

Once again, Michelle began to question the wisdom of her plan. It seemed straightforward when she'd first voiced it. She'd help Josh, he'd help her. But Penny was an unknown in the equation. What would this arrangement do to her?

Dinner went well. Michelle wondered if Josh had a talk with Penny before they came to the restaurant. She was the model of propriety. When Michelle commented on it, Josh smiled smugly.

"So, tell me, how did you manage? Quite a difference from the doughnut place," Michelle said.

"Told her she could bring her bear."

"The teddy bear?"

He nodded. "Usually I don't let her bring him everywhere with her. She's old enough to go out in public without it. But I let her bring him on the condition that she was a very good girl."

"Bribery."

He nodded smugly. "Works every time."

"I'll remember that."

When they finished eating, Michelle suggested they try one of the major department stores on Canal Street. The children's department was large and offered a wide variety of clothes. She found two dresses immediately that she thought would be appropriate for Penny.

"Which one do you like?" she asked the little girl.

Penny had retreated to her dad's side and looked at the dresses suspiciously.

"I like the blue one," Josh said nudging his daughter.

"I like both the blue and the pink. Which do you like, Penny?" Michelle asked again.

Penny pointed to the blue one.

"Let's go try it on, shall we?" Michelle asked, replacing the pink one on the rack.

"Don't gots to," Penny said, clutching her bear tighter.

"Don't have to," Michelle corrected. "Don't say got, Penny, say have. And I think you'll look very pretty in this dress. You can try it on and show your daddy. Want to?"

Penny shook her head.

Michelle looked at Josh for help, but he just watched her with amused interest.

Frustrated, she knew this was some kind of test. But she hadn't a clue how to deal with children. Spotting the teddy bear, she had an idea.

"I tell you what, Penny. Let's try on the dress to see if it fits and then we'll go find something pretty for your teddy bear. So he'll be all dressed up at the wedding, too."

"Bribery," Josh murmured.

"Okay," Penny said, relinquishing her hold on her father's leg and holding out her hand for Michelle's.

"Whatever works," Michelle said triumphantly.

The sound of Josh's laughter followed them to the dressing rooms. Once there Michelle had another minor skirmish in getting Penny to remove her hat. When she saw the chopped-off hair, Michelle began to understand why Penny wanted to wear her hat all the time.

She looked adorable in the dress, despite the baseball cap she'd insisted in putting on once the dress was buttoned.

"Go show your daddy how pretty you look," Michelle said with a smile.

When Penny darted from the stall, Michelle picked up the bear, wondering where they could find clothes for him. He was a bit ragged, obviously from years of loving.

Penny rushed back in, her face smiling. "Daddy said I look like a fairy princess."

"And so you do. We'll take the dress home and you can wear it on Saturday."

Penny pirouetted before the mirror for several minutes before allowing Michelle to unfasten and remove the dress. Once again wearing her shorts, shirt and baseball cap, they left to find Josh.

As they waited for the clerk to ring up the sale, Michelle moved near Josh.

"Where does Penny get her hair cut?" she asked softly.

He looked sheepish. "I cut it. She hates barber shops."

"Barber shops? Josh, she should go to a shop that caters for children."

He looked at her for a long moment, then nodded. "You were right at the beginning. I do need a wife. You can take her there, buy her clothes, and do all the things for a little girl that I don't have a clue about."

"Your daughter looks darling in the dress," the sales clerk told Michelle.

She started to correct the woman, then just smiled. In only a few days, technically Penny would be her stepdaughter. For a moment, Michelle tried to consider all the changes she'd find in her life. It seemed like a lot all at once. But she couldn't lose sight of the reason for the charade.

For a moment she let herself imagine marrying forever. To bind her life with Josh's. Maybe they'd have children of their own. And if that happened, they'd outgrow his house and need a larger one. Nothing as ostentatious or cold as Talmadge Hall, but a big house full of laughter and love.

"Ready?" Josh said, shattering the daydream.

"Sure. We need to find something for the bear."

Daydreams had no place in their business arrangement.

Luck was with them, Michelle felt, when they found a cute vest and top hat with a little elastic chin strap for the bear in the toy department. Penny was ecstatic and carefully carried her bear proudly.

"Now if we can get her hair trimmed, we'll be all set," Michelle said. It was getting late. It would be dark before long.

"What time does Penny go to bed?"

"Usually around eight. But since there's no child care for her to go tomorrow, she can sleep in."

"First thing in the morning, I'll see if I can find a hair salon that specializes in kids. Can you take her if I do?"

"Depends on the time. Try to make an afternoon appointment. She comes with me to the office each day, but we're not there all day. She gets bored or into mischief."

"Did you find another secretary?"

"Not yet. But I have a temp in who at least answers the phones and does some rudimentary typing. Is your offer to help still open?"

Michelle nodded.

"Maybe next week I might take you up on it. Though I'm hoping my being in the office without Penny will give me enough time to get caught up."

"I've told Personnel about my marriage and already preregistered Penny for the day care starting on Monday."

"I've already assigned one of my operatives to canvass the fifty states looking for any records they can find for your father. We have his name and age—we'll find him."

Michelle nodded, pleased that Josh had already started the ball rolling in locating her father even before their mock wedding.

What if he found him almost immediately? She was committed to this marriage at least until Caroline had her baby.

Josh dropped Michelle at home, but refused her invitation to come up for coffee. He had to get Penny home and into bed.

When Michelle let herself into her apartment, she was surprised to find the lights on.

"Hello?"

"Hey, Michelle. Where have you been?" Abby was lounging on the sofa, watching TV. She sprang up when her sister entered the living room. "I let myself in when you didn't answer the bell."

"I didn't know you were coming over," Michelle said, giving her sister a brief hug.

"Out with Josh?" Abby guessed, her eyes twinkling.

"Yes, we went to dinner."

"I guess that answers one question," Abby said, turning to cut off the TV.

"What question?" Michelle asked, tossing her purse on a chair and sinking down in another. She was tired.

How long was Abby planning to stay?

"Whether you and Josh are sleeping together already."

Heat stole into her cheeks. Michelle tried to look indignant, but the image that danced before her eyes made that difficult.

"No, we are not!" she said.

The feelings that swamped her couldn't be disappointment. She hardly knew the man. Certainly not enough to sleep with him! Though, of course, her sisters didn't know that. They thought she and Josh were wildly in love and impatient to be married.

"You needn't sound so indignant. Engaged people do sometimes anticipate the marriage vows these days. Anyway, I'm glad I don't have to dash out in order to avoid being a fifth wheel. But I'm sorry I didn't get to meet him. Caroline said he's very tall and has a great sense of humor. But we're both surprised at the suddenness of it all."

"I am, too, if you want the truth." But not the entire truth, of course, Michelle thought.

She had to keep the pretense for Abby as well as Caroline. Her sister rarely thought before she spoke and Michelle didn't want to take the chance Abby would spill the beans to Caroline.

"But you're sure about this?" Abby pressed, looking serious.

"I'm sure." Michelle said with conviction.

It was a mutually beneficial arrangement. Josh would keep Penny instead of sending her to live with grandparents. Michelle knew how important it was that the little girl didn't have to grow up without a father.

And sooner or later Josh would locate Sam Williams, of that Michelle was certain. If he attacked his cases as he did his personal life, she knew Josh must be wildly successful.

"Then the next thing is what can I do to help? I've taken the next three days off from work to help with anything you need."

"Oh, Abby, you didn't have to do that. But thanks. I think I've got everything lined up, but you know how things can go wrong at the last minute."

Michelle explained what she'd arranged for the

ceremony, showed her sister the suit she'd bought for the event and discussed the luncheon reservations she'd made.

Remembering Josh's adage about playing a role, she tried to include his name in the conversation as often as she could. And each time, she felt her heart skip a beat. The man was positively dangerous—even in absentia. Abby seemed completely convinced of the reality of her sister's devotion for the man. Michelle couldn't wait to tell him. She wanted some of that praise he so freely gave his daughter.

"You haven't said a word about your honeymoon. Where are you going?" Abby asked some time later.

Michelle froze for a moment. She should have anticipated that question. Especially after her sister and Brandon had taken a second honeymoon for a few days after they renewed their vows.

"Actually, I have taken so much time off dealing with helping wind up Grandmother's estate, that I don't have a lot of time left. And Josh is really busy with a new case, so we've decided to postpone a honeymoon for a while. It'll be enough to be together."

Abby looked at her suspiciously, but her expression cleared in another moment and she grinned. "I guess anywhere the two of you are is good enough for a honeymoon, right?"

Michelle nodded.

"And you'll be moving into his place, did you say?"

"Yes. We'll be moving most of my things this weekend. I've already started packing."

"That's no fun. You two go off somewhere and at least

spend the weekend together. I have a bunch of friends at the hospital who would be happy to help me pack you up and move you. Consider it part of my wedding present."

Good grief, Michelle thought. Her sister would examine every inch of Josh's house and know instantly something was wrong if asked to put Michelle's things in a separate bedroom. How could she get out of this? "I can't let you do that!"

"Nonsense. You can stay at some fancy hotel downtown and just give me the keys to his place. By the time you get there Sunday night, I'll have all your things moved and put away."

"I'll check with Josh," Michelle stalled.

Panic struck. She hoped Josh could come up with a convincing reason to refuse her sister's offer. Michelle obviously wasn't as quick on her feet as he was. She liked order and organization. Josh's very life's career dealt in uncertainties and quick thinking.

Michelle felt exhausted when she went to bed. Abby was sleeping on the couch and planned to stay with her sister until the ceremony. Tomorrow they'd finalize everything and Friday night go to Caroline's for the evening. Michelle knew things were spinning out of control, but she couldn't seem to stop them. Not without giving her family a hint of the true nature of this rushed marriage. And that she refused to do.

At work Thursday morning, Michelle located a children's hair salon which could take Penny on a rush basis. She called Josh. He wasn't at home, so she tried the office.

"O'Malley." His tone was clipped.

"Hi, Josh. I've got some good news and some bad. Which do you want first?"

"If the bad is you've changed your mind, I don't want to hear it. No, Penny, don't touch that!" The receiver banged on the desk. Michelle waited patiently. In just a moment he spoke again.

"Sorry, she was trying the paper cutter. That's all I'd need, to show up Saturday with a kid minus four fingers."

"My bad news is not that I changed my mind."

For a moment she let the knowledge he'd consider that bad to permeate. It was nice.

"Actually in other circumstances it might be considered good. But not in this."

Quickly she outlined Abby's suggestion.

"So what's the problem? We'd owe her big-time because we don't have to move the stuff ourselves."

"Don't you see, she'll think we are sharing a room and move all my stuff into your bedroom."

"And we can't move it out later?"

"You wouldn't mind the disruption?"

The silence on the other end went on for several seconds. Finally, Josh spoke slowly. "You know, Michelle, we might want to think about this for a bit. We'll be married."

Stunned, Michelle gripped the receiver. Was he propositioning her?

"Penny, put that down. Michelle? I've got to cut this short. We can discuss that later. What's the good news?"

"I've found a place that'll cut Penny's hair this afternoon

at one thirty." Reading the address, Michelle was amazed her voice even worked. She wanted to discuss his odd comment now, not at some future date. She found Josh O'Malley absolutely fascinating. Was he suggesting making this marriage real?

Backing away from the tantalizing thoughts of making their marriage something more, Michelle tried to get a grip on her emotions. All brides were emotional. This would pass. And she had obviously misunderstood what he was saying. He'd gone on and on why he didn't believe in marriage any more.

"Okay, I'll take her and if she screams the place down, we'll be sure they have your name!"

Michelle laughed. "She'll be fine. You'll see a world of difference between a beauty parlor and a barber shop. These people cater to kids. They know what they're doing. The experience will be good for you."

"I have all the experience I need right now. Anything else?"

"No, I guess not. You have the address and room for the judge."

"Yep, tucked in my wallet. And the new shoes for Penny. Saturday we'll get dressed early enough that if I can't get the buttons done, I'll go next door to my neighbor. She'll want every detail anyway."

Michelle laughed again. Talking with Josh was always an adventure. And he was wonderful with his daughter. That little girl would never lack for love and attention while she was growing up.

"See you Saturday, babe," Josh said as he hung up.

Michelle grimaced as she replaced the receiver. *Babe* again. Was she going to have to cure him of that like she needed to cure Penny of saying "gots"?

Saturday was a beautiful day, sunny and warm. Caroline prepared a lavish breakfast which she and Abby served Michelle in bed. Then they both promptly sat on the spread and shared the feast.

"This is like when we were kids," Caroline said, nibbling on a slice of bread coated with marmalade.

"Yes, only we don't have to worry about Grandmother storming in and ruining everything," Abby said.

"No, she ruined everything long ago when she ran our father off," Michelle said.

Caroline and Abby looked at her.

"I vaguely remember him, but you were so young, I didn't think you'd miss him that much," Caroline said slowly.

"I didn't have to know him to miss him. Remember all the school events when parents attended? Not just the recitals that Grandmother came to, but the soccer events, or the May Day carnival? I was always so envious of girls whose fathers swung them up in their arms and hugged them. I imagined them playing ball, or tag or something in their yards on weekends. Or going on picnics or even just sitting together on a sofa and reading."

"So it wasn't just me who missed him," Caroline said slowly.

"No, it wasn't," Abby said. "I'd have loved to have both our parents. Once I learned Grandmother was the reason our father left, I couldn't help wondering about Mom. Did she just give up? Of course I don't remember either of them but I have to wonder that if Eugenia hadn't interfered, would both of our parents still be alive and close by?"

The three sisters were silent for a long moment, until Caroline looked around and then smiled brightly.

"Hey, no long faces. We have a wedding to attend today! Aren't you thrilled to death, Michelle?"

Remembering her role, Michelle threw herself into it enthusiastically. Neither sister would ever suspect the true reason. Time enough to explain everything after Caroline's baby was safely born and the mock marriage to Josh had ended.

Dressing in the creamy-white silk suit, Michelle was delighted with the way she looked. Something caused her eyes to sparkle and her skin to glow with subtle color. She sat quietly while Abby fussed with her hair, pleased with the resulting cascade of curls that looked perfect with the jaunty little hat and veil.

"Here, this was Mother's." Caroline handed her a locket. "It's old and borrowed."

"Here, this is blue." Abby handed her a ruffly garter. "And I know Josh will love removing it to toss."

"Abby, there are only going to be about six people there. Not enough to fuss with such traditions."

"If there is one bachelor, that's enough."

When they walked into the living room, Brandon rose. Wearing a dark suit with snowy white shirt, he looked the epitome of a successful entrepreneur. Michelle smiled at him. He made her sister so happy, she'd always cherish him for that.

Would she ever find a love so strong one day?

"We're ready," Caroline said. Her maternity dress was pure elegance—and not far different in style from the wedding gown she'd worn only a few weeks earlier for the renewal of their vows.

"Wait, we need a lucky penny," Abby said.

"Allow me," Brandon said, reaching into his trousers. He brought out a gold coin. "I've had this since I found it as a kid on the bayou. It's brought me luck over the years. Let's hope it does for you, too, Michelle."

"Thank you." Her eyes met those of every one filming over with tears. "I'm so glad you're my family."

"And in a few more hours we'll add another with Josh."

"Oh, dear," Michelle said. "I forgot to tell you about Penny."

"Who?"

"Josh's daughter. Penny's four. She'll be joining the family, too."

"He has a kid? You're going to be a stepmother? And you are only telling us now?" Abby asked.

Caroline shook her head. "Abby, you idiot, she's in love with Josh. That he has a child is an extra bonus, but her mind's on him. I can understand. Let's go. I can't wait to meet her. We don't want to be late. I wouldn't expect a lot of traffic on a Saturday, but you never know."

The judge's chambers looked crowded when Michelle entered. For a moment she almost panicked. Then reason took control. She went to greet two of her coworkers—both longtime friends. She'd invited them to allay any suspicions Caroline might have had. Then she greeted a man and woman she didn't know, Josh's employees. Glancing at her watch, she noted it was almost the agreed time.

Nervous, she spoke with the judge and checked the door. Where was Josh? He hadn't changed *his* mind, had he?

Just before noon, he entered, carrying Penny on one arm and a big bouquet of flowers in the other hand. The child looked adorable. Her hair was cut short as a pixie with a blue ribbon bow centered on the top. Her dress did make her look like a fairy princess, Michelle thought, smiling at the child with affection. She felt as proud of how sweet Penny looked as if she were truly her mother.

Then her gaze moved to Josh and she stood still. He looked fantastic. His charcoal gray suit and pale blue shirt fit as though they'd been made especially for him. They emphasized his broad shoulders, his height, and the darkness of his tan. She forced in a breath and moved closer, aware of only Josh in the gathering of friends and relatives.

"You made it," she said inanely.

"Thanks to Mrs. Turner across the street. These buttons are too tiny!"

Michelle's sisters immediately joined them. She introduced Abby and was surprised when Abby held out her arms to see Penny lean right into them.

"I'll hold this pretty girl while the ceremony takes place. Then we'll sit together at lunch. Want to do that, Penny?"

"Wif my bear?"

"Sure thing, sugar."

"Where are the bear and the cap?" Michelle asked.

"They're both in the car. Penny gets to have them as soon as we leave here," Josh said, holding out the flowers. "These are for you. A bride needs more than a corsage."

As soon as she took them he reached out to draw her into his arms. Without another word, he kissed her long and hard.

Michelle was acutely conscious of every person in the room staring at them. She knew he was playing his role, but for a moment let herself float on the sensations that swept through her. And wished it were for real as she kissed him back.

"Dearly Beloved—" the judge began a few minutes later.

Josh stood in front of the man and tried not to let the words remind him of another time. This marriage would be nothing like his first one. He glanced at Michelle, disconcerted to find her standing rigid, her solemn gaze fixed on him. Slowly he winked, pleased to note the hint of color that flooded her cheeks. Gradually she relaxed. He wished he could.

But the situation was too fraught with problems. How could he have agreed to another marriage? Hadn't the problems before been enough to ensure he never tried it again?

Michelle was different from Sylvia, a small voice reminded him. And the circumstances were totally different. He'd have to remember that.

Glancing around quickly, he looked at Michelle's sisters. They didn't look alike, except for the Talmadge blue eyes. Caroline had dark hair while Abby's was a honey-blond. He liked Michelle's rich auburn color the best.

How would they all take this mock marriage when the truth was revealed?

"Do you, Josh—"

He had to pay attention. Time enough later to figure out how he'd convinced himself this was a good idea.

Chapter Five

"I now pronounce you man and wife. You may kiss your bride," the judge finished.

Josh took full advantage. Michelle's eyes widened as he pulled her into his embrace. She had a knack of always looking so surprised when he touched her or said something the slightest bit provocative. Unfortunately, the trait only had him finding more ways to surprise her to see that reaction.

Her lips were warm and soft. Whatever else, he liked kissing her. Far too much, he thought a moment later when he pulled back to the gentle laughter of their guests. Yet it seemed too brief.

Michelle's face flamed with color. Feeling a certain sense of satisfaction to have caused that reaction, Josh grinned and turned to face the others.

"Congratulations!" someone called.

In no time, their friends and family surged around to offer felicitations and hugs. Josh endured them good-naturedly. At least for the time being he had his personal life under some control. Michelle would take care of Penny for him and let him concentrate on business.

Playing the role of devoted husband wouldn't be a

hardship. He threaded his fingers through hers and smiled, liking the feelings he experienced around Michelle. Except for a certain state of awareness that he hadn't experienced since he'd been a teenager.

"Welcome to the family," Abby said as she reached up to give him a hug, Penny between them. "We got a double bonus today, with both you and Penny. She's a sweetheart."

Penny beamed at her father. "This is Auntie Abby."

"I know she is."

For a moment the term threw him. Doubt rose. Was he doing the right thing for Penny? Would she become attached to Michelle and her family? They were nice people, and without letting them know of the temporary nature of this marriage, would they become too much a part of their lives only to be missed when the marriage ended?

Maybe he shouldn't have agreed to Michelle's request for the entire charade.

Before he could think more along those lines, Bethany, one of Michelle's friends from work, brought out her camera and began to organize a series of poses of the wedding party. Then the entire group moved to one of the restaurants nearby where Michelle had made reservations.

The luncheon was perfect. The guests brought gifts which were piled on a table against the wall. Toasts were offered to the newly married couple. Abby and Caroline had arranged for a wedding cake. Penny was enchanted with the small man and woman on top and claimed them for her own once the cake had been cut. She had her bear in tow, but had left the cap in the car.

"This is for you," Caroline said, slipping an envelope to Michelle as she and Brandon came over when the guests were getting ready to leave. "We didn't want to put it with the other gifts for fear you wouldn't open it until tomorrow or something."

"What is it?"

Caroline smiled broadly. "Brandon and I are treating you both for a night at Le Carillon," she said. "Abby said she and her friends are moving your things to Josh's this weekend, so we thought we'd treat tonight at the hotel. And I want to keep Penny, if she'll come. Get me some practice."

Michelle's mind spun. She looked at Josh in panic. They'd done nothing about Abby's plans to move her things. Now this. What could she do without giving away the reason for their arrangement? The terms of this marriage?

Caroline waited expectantly. Taking a deep breath, Michelle smiled. She hugged Caroline and then Brandon. "Wow, this is so great! Thank you. I didn't expect anything like this."

Desperately she sought for a reason to decline, but none came to mind.

Josh put his arm around Michelle and added his thanks. "We couldn't take a honeymoon just yet, but this will be a start. We appreciate it."

The touch of his arm on her shoulder almost short-circuited Michelle's brain. She was aware of every inch of the man, of his rumbling laughter, of his muscles as he leaned forward a bit to shake Brandon's hand, the warmth that radiated and enveloped her. How could anyone be expected to make decisions when thoughts of kisses and caresses dominated?

"We'll help you take the gifts home. We can then pack something for Penny and be off," Caroline said.

"I expect both you and Penny could use a nap," Brandon said.

"You're right. But this has been a wonderful day!"

Michelle's cheeks ached with her smile. She felt like such a fraud. But it was for a good cause, she reminded herself. Josh would locate their father. And she'd make sure sweet little Penny was able to remain with hers.

The room at Le Carillon was luxurious, as would be expected from one of New Orleans' five-star hotels. With a view of the old French Quarter and the slow-moving Mississippi River beyond, it appealed to the senses in every way. Bright blossoms filled vases around the sitting room. The thick carpet had Michelle wanting to slip off her shoes and walk barefoot. The muted colors blended with a soothing elegance.

When the bellman left, Michelle turned to look at Josh. They were alone in this lovely suite, and had to stay until morning!

"I didn't know how to get out of it," she began.

"Not without revealing all to your sister and brother-in-law," he agreed, walking around examining the furnishings. Stopping by the window, he looked at the view.

"And Abby, she means well, too."

"You're lucky to have a close family. They're happy for you and want to share that happiness."

"I know. I feel like such a fraud."

Josh turned around, leaned against the glass, his hands in the pockets of his trousers. "Why?"

"They think this is real."

"The marriage is real."

She looked surprised. "Yes, it is, isn't it? But I mean they think we're in love and will stay together forever. All the people at the wedding thought it was real. What do we do with all the wedding presents?"

"Write thank-you notes?"

Michelle frowned and moved to sink down on the sofa. "We got them under false pretenses."

Josh shook his head. "Michelle, we got married. We'll stay married at least for several months. The people we invited today were happy to share in what they thought was a special day for us. Let them have the fun of giving gifts. If your sensibilities won't allow it, when we split, you can return them."

She let Josh's words wash through her. Idly tracing the pattern on the sofa fabric, she admitted she was trying to find something to talk about. She was more concerned about spending the night in this hotel suite alone with Josh, rather than the wedding presents.

What would they talk about? It was hours until morning. Even if they went out to dinner and a movie or something, she wasn't sure she could last until time to leave tomorrow.

If it had been someone else, maybe. But she was growing more and more interested in the man who'd just become her husband. He was totally different from anyone else she knew.

Not that she knew him that well.

Venturing a glance in his direction, she was startled to find him staring at her.

"What?"

"Just thinking. Want to change into something more comfortable? I do."

She nodded, wondering with a touch of trepidation if he expected them to change together in the bedroom.

He pushed away and went toward the bedroom door. "I'll change, then leave it to you."

Pausing at the doorway, he looked over his shoulder. "You look lovely in your suit and hat. I'm glad your friend took those pictures."

Michelle felt the breath leave her at that statement. The door closed and she leaned back on the sofa, feeling confused and flustered. He was glad for the pictures? She thought he'd endured the process just to further their charade.

Smiling, she remembered Bethany's insistence on all the different poses: she and Josh, she, Josh and Penny, pictures with the judge, with her sisters, and several group shots with everyone.

For a second, Michelle wistfully wished it had been a real wedding. One meant to last.

Sighing, she rose and crossed to the window, her ears attuned toward the bedroom. When Josh finished changing, she'd take off her wedding finery.

Maybe they could go for a walk or something. She felt restless and unsettled and far too fascinated with the man in the next room.

An hour later they strolled along the river. Michelle sought for something to talk about, but felt as tongue-tied as a teenager on a first date. She cleared her throat.

"Did you get a chance to talk to Edith Strong yet?" she asked.

He shook his head. "No, I tried calling, but she couldn't come to the phone at that time. I thought we could ride up one day and see her together. She knows you and will likely be more forthcoming if you're there."

"Okay."

Silence. The hot Louisiana sun beat down on them. Only a slight breeze blew from the water which did little to cool the air.

Josh reached for her arm, turning her toward a vacant bench in the shade of an old oak.

"Let's sit and talk."

Michelle nodded, nerves stretched taut. "About what?"

Josh waited until they sat, then looked out across the water. "About us and this marriage."

She cleared her throat. "Okay."

Her heart thrummed in her chest, her hands grew damp and she wiped them surreptitiously on her skirt.

"I'll be blunt. I'm attracted to you, Michelle. You must have recognized that. I didn't expect it and didn't want it, but there it is."

"That's blunt," she blurted out, her eyes wide as she stared at Josh. What did he want her to say?

He grimaced slightly, then gave her a half smile. "Yeah, well, that's the best way, I think. The thing is, I didn't plan to marry again. My relationship with Sylvia wasn't the best recommendation for a second try."

"I remember you didn't exactly leap at the chance to get married when I first brought it up."

"I appreciate what you're doing for Penny. And me. I don't know how I could have managed without this arrangement. And the last thing I wanted was to send her away. So maybe the next to last thing I wanted was to get involved again."

"Involved?"

He reached out to trace a finger along her cheek, as if fascinated by the texture of her skin.

"You're so soft," he said slowly.

Heat rushed through Michelle at his touch. Heat and a yearning that grew stronger each time she was with Josh.

"What is it you want, Josh?"

"I want you, Michelle O'Malley."

The world spun. Michelle gripped the edge of the bench to keep from flying off. Had she heard him correctly?

"I know we planned on a platonic relationship. And I'll stick with that, if you like. But I don't think this attraction is all one-sided and I wanted you to know where I stand." He dropped his hand and turned, arms crossed, to gaze at the river.

"I don't know quite what to say," she said a few second later. The silence seemed to reverberate.

"You don't have to say anything unless you want to agree to an affair while we're married."

She smiled. "An affair while we are married, that sounds weird."

He looked at her and shrugged. "Temporary like this marriage. What would you call it?"

She swallowed. He was serious. *He wanted her!* Oh wow!

"We don't even know each other very well."

"So we did it backwards, got married, then learned about each other. What do you want to know?"

"Everything." Michelle surprised herself with the intensity of her curiosity. She wanted to learn every scrap of information she could about Josh.

"Where you were born, grew up. Where your parents are now? What you were like as a little boy? What made you become a private investigator?"

He stretched out his feet and settled on the bench. "Short version: born here in New Orleans. I have two brothers, neither of whom live here now. One's in New York, the other in L.A. My folks are both dead, died in the hurricane. No grandparents living, but they were all around when I was a kid. The only other relatives Penny has are her mother's parents in Atlanta. I went to school at Tulane, got a law degree, decided I liked investigating more than prosecuting or defending, so switched from practicing law to detective work." He arched an eyebrow as his gaze met hers. "Anything more?"

"That's short, all right."

"So tell me your life story."

"In twenty-five words or less?"

"In as many words as you need."

"What don't you already know from your investigation of my background?"

"Whether you've ever been in love. Why you aren't married. Why you moved to New Orleans right after high school."

"I thought I was in love once—in high school. I am married now—to you. And I left Baton Rouge as soon as I could to escape my domineering grandmother."

"And no current boyfriend?"

She shook her head.

Josh was silent for a long moment. "Have you ever had an affair before?"

Michelle shook her head again.

"So that wide-eyed innocent act isn't really an act at all?"

"What wide-eyed innocent act?"

"Never mind. I've put my cards on the table. You let me know if you want to pick them up."

"Josh, I don't think having an affair is such a good idea. This is just a temporary arrangement while you locate my father. We don't want to complicate things."

Michelle tried for a calm rational argument, but her heart was still racing out of control and a major part of her wanted to throw herself into his arms and agree to any terms he wanted.

But where would that leave her when it came time to end their marriage? She was already fascinated by the man. If there was any physical intimacy between them would she endanger her heart as well?

He rose. "If you change your mind, you let me know. Come on, I want to walk."

The rest of the afternoon spun by. Michelle was worried

at first that Josh would push her to comply with his outrageous suggestion. But he never even hinted. They were simply two people thrown together by circumstances who had to spend time together. He questioned her about her father, trying to gather as much information as she could provide.

Then they spoke of Penny, of the renovations in the downtown area, and of the chances of the Saints for next year's Super Bowl.

When they returned to their suite after dinner, Josh located the television and turned it on.

"The sofa folds out into a bed. I'll take that," he said as he kicked off his shoes.

Michelle was touched. Had he seen how nervous she was?

"Thank you. I think I'll go to bed now, if you don't mind. It's been a long day." And she hadn't slept all that well the night before.

"Let me get my suitcase."

Ten minutes later Michelle slipped beneath the cool sheets and turned off the light. She could hear the low murmur of the television. For a moment she wondered if she was doing right to resist his offer of an affair. They were married. And she hadn't met anyone in her life she felt drawn to as much as Josh. Normally shy and uncertain, she felt she was growing more comfortable in his company. Who knew if she'd ever find a man to fall in love with and marry. Maybe she should take Josh up on his offer.

Josh was already up and dressed and raring to go when Michelle came out of the bedroom the next morning.

"I miss Penny," he said with a sheepish grin. "This is only the second night we've been apart since she came to live with me last year. I had a trip last March I couldn't avoid when I had one of the revolving housekeepers watch her."

"Don't you want to eat, first?" Michelle asked, touched at his revelation.

Josh glanced at his watch, and nodded. "It's a bit early. We wouldn't want Caroline to think we didn't enjoy the present."

"Thanks for going along with all that. We're counting on her having a fine healthy baby. I sure don't want to add any worry at this stage. She's nervous enough as it is."

"Chances should be good that the baby will be fine."

"So her doctor says."

"Tell me more about Abby. Penny sure took to her yesterday."

Michelle nodded, feeling just a hint of the jealousy that had hit her yesterday. She wanted Penny to like her, but they had never hit it off as well as the instant rapport between Abby and the little girl. She told Josh how her sister had chosen nursing as her vocation, and the genuine feelings for others she had.

They ordered breakfast and Michelle talked more about her sisters, inadvertently giving Josh a glimpse into her life at her grandmother's. He added comments comparing his childhood with hers and she gleaned a broader perspective of his own background.

When they picked up Penny, she wore her blue ribbon instead of the baseball cap, and carried her dressed-up teddy bear. She gave Caroline and Brandon huge hugs and waved all the way down the street as they headed for Josh's house.

On the ride, Penny spoke almost nonstop about staying with Auntie Caroline and Unca Brandon. Michelle smiled at her chatter, hoping Penny would soon feel as comfortable with her as she did with her sisters.

When they arrived home, Josh carried the two small overnight cases into his bedroom. Michelle followed, carrying her wedding outfit. Standing near the bed, he surveyed the room. Except for a few items on the dresser, it didn't look different from when he left. But striding to the closet and opening the door, he saw dresses, skirts and blouses hanging side by side with his own suits. Colorful high heels competed for floor space with his own dark shoes.

"I'll move everything into the other room," Michelle said, coming to stand beside him. "If you and Penny want to play out back as she suggested, I can do it now."

He reached out a finger and tilted her chin. Brushing his lips across hers, he then looked into her eyes.

"Remember what I said, you just give the word."

Flustered, Michelle nodded, longing to throw caution to the wind and at least consider his amazing suggestion. With dazed eyes, she watched him stride from the room and call Penny.

Soon the sound of childish laughter came in through the open window. Michelle detoured by the window, her arms full of dresses, to look out. Josh was playing ball with Penny. He'd gently lob the big ball toward the little girl's outstretched hands. The ball would actually bounce against one palm or the other, then fall to the grass. Laughing, she'd race to pick it up and throw it back to her father. Once in a while, Josh managed to run fast enough to catch an erratic toss.

Both of them appeared to be having a wonderful time.

Wistfully Michelle watched for long moments. Penny was one lucky little girl. She'd have wonderful memories growing up. Once again the sense of rightness filled her. If nothing else, Michelle was glad she'd made this possible.

But she felt oddly left out. Josh hadn't included her.

Sighing softly, she carried her dresses to her room.

Monday morning Josh left early. Penny was still eating breakfast. Michelle had dressed for work before preparing the meal, so she was ready. As soon as Penny was finished, they'd leave for the office and Penny's new day care center.

"Hurry up, Penny. We need to leave soon," Michelle said as the child dawdled over her milk.

"Don't gots to," Penny mumbled. She wore her baseball hat today, and her teddy bear waited on the floor beside her chair.

"Don't have to. Don't say got, say have." Michelle murmured, checking the time again.

She planned to drive to work rather than subject Penny to the bus, but wasn't sure how heavy the traffic would be from Josh's house. She wanted to leave plenty of time to take Penny to the day care and still make it on time to her desk.

"Are you finished with your milk?"

"No." She fiddled with the glass.

"Penny, we have to go."

Penny's lower lip pushed out and she glared at Michelle. "Don't gots to."

"Yes, you do have to. You're going to a new day care today. We need to be there on time. Come on."

"No!" Penny scooted off her chair, snatched up her bear and ran for her room.

Michelle stared after her for a long moment. Josh had said she was a handful sometimes. Had she or her sisters ever behaved like that with their grandmother? Somehow she doubted it.

She put everything in the car and went to get Penny. Maybe she'd call Abby later and ask for pointers. "Come on, Penny. Time to go."

"Don't gots to," Penny stated from her position on her bed. She had her back to the door.

Michelle crossed the room and knelt beside the bed, trying to catch Penny's eye. "I'll tell you what. If you come now like a good girl, we'll stop at the park on the way home. How about that?"

Warily Penny studied Michelle. After a long moment, she nodded and crawled to the edge of the bed. "Okay. I can go on the swing?"

"Yes."

Relieved they were heading out, Michelle ignored the bribery aspect, though her own words echoed in her mind. Right now she was looking for whatever worked. Once she and Penny got to know each other, she'd know better how to deal with the child. And there was no reason Josh should ever find out about today's bribe.

Josh checked out the front window for the eighteenth time in the last half hour. Where were they? He knew Michelle normally left work at five. Had she had to work late? Couldn't she have called? What if they'd been in a traffic accident? It didn't take ninety minutes to drive from her office building to the house.

He paced the living room, checking his watch again. He'd already called her office, but reached only a recording announcing the office hours. He didn't dare call Caroline, Michelle's admonitions about protecting her sister were too strong. Abby would be at work. He remembered her talking about her days off and how she had switched with others to get the weekend off.

Where were they?

A car turned into the driveway. Rushing to the door, he flung it wide open and stepped outside. Michelle released Penny from the car seat in back, leaning in through the open door. The relief to see them both safe mingled with the attraction he felt for his new wife. He wanted to yell at her for putting him through this worry, then snatch her close and kiss her breathless.

Instead, he clenched his fists and waited with what patience he could muster as they came toward him.

Penny ran ahead, her teddy bear bumping against her leg. "Hi Daddy. I went on the swings. I went really high." She flung herself into his arms when he stooped to her level. Lifting her, he hugged her close.

"Where have you two been?" he demanded when Michelle drew closer.

"We stopped at the park." She looked at him closely. "Is something wrong?"

"You scare the h—" he glanced at his daughter. "You scared me when you weren't home when I arrived. I thought you left work at five."

"I did. Penny and I stopped at the park." She bit her lip as a look of contrition crossed her face. "I'm sorry, Josh, I didn't even think you might be home or worried. I'm not used to living with anyone. And I guess I thought you'd work later than me."

He couldn't help himself. Reaching for her with his free hand, he drew her close enough to kiss. Just the touch of her lips against his sent his temperature soaring. He wondered if she'd given any thought to his proposal.

"You do now! Maybe I overreacted, but I was worried when you both weren't home where I expected you to be," he said, releasing her and turning toward the open door.

"I'll call next time," she said breathlessly.

Josh smiled. At least he got the kissing part right. But if he weren't holding Penny in one arm, he would have done a lot more of that.

"I have a cell phone, you have the number. Maybe we should discuss expectations. I thought you'd be here. When you weren't, I got worried."

"I'm sorry. We were fine, weren't we, Penny?"

The little girl nodded and smiled at her father. "I went high on the swing."

"Good for you. What else did you do at the park?"

"Tell your Daddy all we did, Penny. I'm going to change and then start dinner."

Josh listened with half an ear to Penny's excited chatter as he watched Michelle take the stairs to the second story. He hadn't only been worried about Penny, but about Michelle as well. Which didn't make sense. She'd been right on Saturday, they hardly knew each other.

So why did the thought of her in any trouble bring out all the protective instincts he possessed?

Chapter Six

Michelle changed, feeling odd. It'd been a long time since anyone had worried about where she was. There was obviously more to this marriage than she originally anticipated. But it felt nice. At first she thought Josh had been concerned solely about Penny. Not so. He'd been worried about her as well.

When she went to the kitchen, she saw the two of them in the backyard again. The weather had cooled and it probably felt good to play outside. And Penny sure had enough energy for it. If Josh could run some of that excess energy off, the child would sleep well tonight.

As Michelle prepared a light supper, she tried not to dwell on the kiss Josh had given her when she arrived home. But it was impossible. It had been quick. Over almost before it registered. She wondered what it meant.

Probably relief from the worry that he'd experienced when they hadn't arrived when expected.

Or had there been more in it?

When dinner was ready, she went to the door that led to the yard. For a second she watched Josh and Penny play. Michelle longed to run out and join them, but they looked so in tune with each other she felt like an outsider. Would they want her to join them?

"Dinner's ready," she called.

Josh looked up and waved, scooping up his daughter and jogging toward Michelle.

"We're starving, right Penny?"

The little girl laughed as she clung to her father and nodded. "Starving!"

"Well then it's a good thing I made lots of dinner, isn't it?" Michelle said as they swept past her and headed to the downstairs bathroom to wash up.

For the first time in years, Michelle felt she was part of a family as the three of them sat at the table to eat. Penny told her father all about her first day at the day care and then about their adventure in the park. Josh asked lots of questions and paid close attention to every word.

His gaze met Michelle's on more than one occasion. He'd smile and wink, as if they had a special code. She hadn't enjoyed a meal so much since she'd been a little girl having supper with just her two sisters.

"I've brought a ton of work home. The records and billing are a mess. After Penny's in bed, I'll take you up on your offer of some help, if you're not too tired," he said as they finished eating.

Michelle nodded, feeling even more included. "That's fine, I don't feel tired at all."

Full of energy and excited described how she felt.

Michelle loved organizing things. She'd already rearranged a few items in the kitchen to make it more efficient. While Josh was bathing Penny, she plunged into the stack of papers he'd shown her. Everything was mixed up and she had to skim each sheet to get an idea of what it was. But soon she had several distinct piles of reports, invoices, correspondence and legal papers.

"Michelle?" Josh called from upstairs.

"Yes?"

"Can you come tell Penny good-night?"

Jumping up, she hurried to the stairs, a warm glow beginning to spread through her. She'd told Penny good-night when she went up for her bath, but to be requested to come when she was tucked in bed was different.

She entered Penny's room and smiled at the little girl all tucked up in her bed.

"Good night, sweetie. I hope you sleep well."

"Kissy?" Penny said, holding up her arms.

Michelle's heart melted. She crossed the room and drew the child close, relishing her fresh scent, the soft sweetness she cuddled in her arms. Kissing her cheek she laid her back down and tucked her teddy bear near her.

"Tomorrow we'll go to day care again. I'm glad you liked it."

"And have eggs for breakfast?"

"Sure, eggs for breakfast. Nighty-night."

Josh had already left the room by the time Michelle rose. She switched off the light, but left the door ajar as she went in search of him. Wanting to dance down the hall at the change in Penny's attitude, she nevertheless maintained a dignified walk. Her grandmother had always believed any bursts of enthusiasm or wild rejoicing were unladylike. And it was hard sometimes to let go of old taboos.

Josh lounged on the sofa with one of the stacks of papers on his lap. He lay down the sheet he'd been reading when Michelle entered.

"All set?"

"I think she'll be asleep in seconds. That was nice."

"What?"

"That she wanted me to kiss her good-night."

He shrugged and picked up the paper again. "She is a bit cautious around strangers, but she'll warm up to you."

"She took to Abby immediately," Michelle said without thinking.

He raised an eyebrow. "Jealous?"

Smiling sheepishly, she nodded. "I guess I am. Dumb, huh?"

His gaze was serious. "I don't think so. You want her to like you and she's been difficult. Of course Auntie Abby's relationship will be different. And Abby has a totally different personality from you."

"More fun."

"Certainly more lighthearted. Lighten up a bit, Michelle. You're too young to be so serious."

"I've always been serious."

"So kick over the traces and try something different."

"I'll take your advice under advisement."

Josh laughed. "Do as you like. I don't want you to change too much, you're all right as you are." He began reading again.

Michelle sank on a nearby chair, her knees feeling decidedly weak. As compliments went, it sure hadn't been spectacular, but to her, it sounded wonderful.

For a long time there was silence in the room as they each worked. Once Michelle had sorted all the papers, she took a pile and put it in chronological order. The work was not difficult, basic record retention. But from the stack of papers, she knew Josh's business was behind in billings, and in responding to some of his clients. He needed to catch up soon or it would definitely impact the bottom line.

Michelle said good-night sometime later. Josh was still working his way through a stack of papers, jotting notes in the margins, or attaching sheets with his scribble on it.

As she prepared for bed, she again thought of his wild proposal on Saturday. What would it be like to give in to the fantasies that filled her nights? To make love with Josh? She didn't have any experience. She was twenty-five years old. Was there some special man out there for her or was she destined to remain alone once this marriage ended?

She hadn't thought much about it before. Now she thought about it all the time.

Especially since Josh told her he wanted her to change the terms of their business marriage.

The kisses they shared would only be the beginning. And she knew she could scarcely think after one. What would it be like to move on?

Hurriedly brushing her teeth, she dashed down the hall to the safety of her own room. But the closed door didn't shut off the images that danced in her mind. Climbing into bed, she shut her eyes, and relived every kiss the man had given her. It didn't help her at all to fall asleep.

Late Tuesday morning Josh called Michelle. He just wanted to hear her voice.

"Is something wrong?" she asked when he identified himself.

"No. I just wanted to let you know that thanks to you, the temp is able to do more than just answer the phone today. She's typing up several reports and I'll be able to issue invoices once the clients receive their reports."

"Good. You know, if you had a computer at home, we could do some of that work in the evenings to get you caught up even faster."

He was surprised. Sylvia never offered any help. She'd resented his work and time he spent on the job. He frowned. He was not going to compare Michelle with Sylvia. Everything about the two marriages was totally different.

"I suppose I could bring one home from the office," he said slowly. He'd tried to keep work separate from home life, but if Michelle could help him get caught up, he'd be a fool to resist.

"We can work after Penny is in bed each night."

"How did Penny do this morning?"

"Fine. At least today she didn't give me her famous 'don't gots to' routine."

Josh laughed at the dry humor in Michelle's voice. "Bad habit, huh?"

"Josh," Michelle's tone turned mocking. "You have to teach her proper manners so she can take her rightful place in society."

He laughed again. He seemed to do that a lot around Michelle. "That definitely had to be your grandmother's voice."

"Yes. And it sounds funny now, but it didn't when I was growing up. You're lucky I didn't buy into all her lecturing or Penny'd be whisked off to finishing school before you knew it."

"You wouldn't do that to such a little girl." He knew Michelle's heart was too soft.

How had he known that? They hadn't known each other for long. But the way she stood up for his daughter convinced him she was as sweet inside as she appeared on the outside.

"No, I wouldn't. I think it's wonderful she has such a great dad. I'm glad you let me help so you could keep her with you."

Josh studied the clouds through the window. "Is that the only reason you're glad about our marriage?"

He didn't know why he wanted to push the issue, but he wanted something more.

"Of course not. You're going to find my father, aren't you?"

The disappointment surprised him. Those were the terms of their marriage. When he'd told her he wanted a more physical relationship, she hadn't agreed. Nothing had changed from the original agreement.

"Yeah. I'll bring a computer home tonight and we can start catching up on getting some money."

"I'm happy to help," she said quietly.

"Do you plan to go straight home today?"

"Yes. We don't need to stop at the park. I'll tell Penny you called when I see her at lunch."

"You don't have to spend your lunch hour with her every day," Josh said.

"I know, and there will be days when I won't. But that's one of the nice features of having the day care in the building, parents can spend time with their children during the day. It's a good way for us to get to know each other."

He thought of her jealousy of Abby and knew she wanted the extra time to try to establish the same kind of rapport.

"Give her a kiss for me and I'll see you both tonight."

Josh ended the call but didn't move for a long time.

Michelle was proving to be unexpected in more ways than one. Initially he thought she proposed this marriage just to get information on her father. But her attempts to draw closer to Penny and her offers to help him were surprising. Sylvia would never have done such a thing.

In fact, Sylvia had complained long and hard about any extra hours he put in and then complained about the lack of money when he didn't. She liked to play and had never been content with what he provided. She had been a good mother, but wanted everything on her terms.

Michelle was quite different, shy and quiet, but generous. And so beautiful it hurt to look at her and not draw her into his arms.

By Friday, they were well entrenched in a definite pattern. Josh called each day just before lunch. He never stayed on the phone long, but made sure he checked on Penny and Michelle.

In the evenings, once Penny was in bed, they worked together to get the business brought up to date. Catching up on the backlog of invoices was the major accomplishment.

Michelle had several suggestions on work flow that Josh tried and discovered they streamlined things a great deal.

He began telling her about some of his cases and she related what she and Penny did at lunchtime, or the frustrations of dealing with one of the partners in the firm.

But in other areas, they made no progress, in Josh's opinion. He made it a point to kiss Michelle when she arrived home each night, hoping she'd give some indication that she'd like to change the status quo. She returned his kisses, but then every night she seemed to deliberately wait until he was engrossed in something before slipping off to bed.

He was growing more and more frustrated. He'd put his cards on the table and had to admit he had expected her to do something about his suggestion. Instead, she seemed to be ignoring the situation entirely. He wondered how much longer he could go on. She was driving him crazy!

He knew she felt the attraction between them. She responded to his kisses like a kid in a candy shop. Then she'd pull back, wide-eyed and breathless. If Penny wasn't always present, he'd demand another kiss and see where it led.

Finishing up early on Friday, Josh was just about ready to leave for home when the phone rang. He'd wanted to get a jump on the traffic, expecting the holiday weekend to clog the roadways.

"Josh, it's Michelle."

"What's wrong?" He could hear the tension in her voice.

"Nothing major, but my car won't start. I was expecting to leave a little early and already have Penny. When I tried to start the engine, it wouldn't. It makes a funny whirring sound."

"I'll be there in a few minutes."

"I'm parked in the lot behind the building. I'll watch for you."

Josh grabbed the folder he had for the Sam Williams search and headed out. Tomorrow he planned to drive to Baton Rouge to interview Edith Strong. Michelle and Penny were going with him. If they left early enough, they'd be in Baton Rouge in time to talk with Edith before lunch.

After they talked with Mrs. Strong, he'd like to take a swing by Talmadge Hall to see where Michelle had grown up. And maybe find out why she had no attachment to the place.

But first, he had to go get his family.

Michelle sat in the hot car, wishing that the air conditioning at least worked. She should have told Josh they'd wait inside.

She hit the steering wheel again. Stupid car. How could it not work? She's planned a fun dinner for them and now they'd be late getting home and she was hot and cranky.

"How much longer?" Penny asked.

"Your daddy will be here soon."

"I'm hot."

"I know, sweetie. I am too." Too late to go back to the office. Surely Josh would be here soon.

It was a half hour after she called before Josh arrived.

She showed him what happened when she tried turning on the car. He had her release the hood and looked under it for a while, wiggling belts, and poking hoses. Finally he slammed down the hood of the car and wiped his hands on a cloth he'd had in his trunk.

"I can't fix it, babe. We'll have to have it towed to a garage."

With the long weekend for Independence Day, Michelle knew it'd be sometime next week before a garage would be able to get to it.

"Rats. It's been making a funny noise for a few weeks, but I thought it would go away," Michelle said in disgust.

He looked at her. "Go away? Usually when things are making a funny noise, it's a symptom something is wrong."

"It made a funny noise a few years ago and then it went away." Maybe she should have said something but she hoped it would just go away.

"Let's go home. I'll call the garage when we get there," Josh said.

Michelle grabbed her purse and then opened the back door to help Penny from her car seat.

"We're riding in Daddy's car tonight, punkin." The little girl had been more patient than Michelle had expected.

"Even though it doesn't look like much, it runs," Josh said as he opened the back door to get the car seat in for

Penny.

Michelle opened the passenger door and frowned. "It didn't squeak," she said in surprise.

Slowly Josh smiled at her. "I told you I'd oil it."

Michelle's pulse rate increased at the sight of that sexy smile. Feeling confused at her feelings she slid into the car and waited while he closed the door. The silent door.

"Thank you," Michelle said softly when Josh slid behind the wheel, touched he'd made a change for her.

"You only have to tell me what you want, Michelle, and I'll do my best to see you get it. And I always do what I say I will."

Tell him what she wanted? Like more kisses? she almost asked. Was there some way she could let him know that she was tempted by his suggestion they take this marriage a bit farther?

Of course, he was probably looking for a declaration of intent. And she was not sure she could give voice to the churning emotions that confused her. Each time he kissed her, she wanted it to go on forever.

If Josh hadn't changed his mind, she had to find a way to let him know she had changed hers without feeling like a brazen hussy.

Turning, her eye caught the folder on the middle of the front seat. The label was clear. It was the one for her father. Feeling like a deflated balloon, she sighed and looked out the front window. She'd better remember exactly why she and Josh had agreed to this marriage. He might want a fling, an affair, but nothing had been said about forever.

And Michelle had a feeling she was a forever kind of person.

When Michelle came down for breakfast the next morning, Penny and her father were already eating cereal for breakfast.

"Going for a ride," Penny said proudly.

"I know that, sweetheart. We're going to the town where I used to live." Michelle smiled at the child, and then Josh, her breath catching at the sight of him. After a week of sharing a house, she should be used to the reaction. But it always caught her by surprise. Trying to get control of her wayward emotions, she popped some bread in the toaster.

He looked wonderful in the light blue shirt and faded jeans—like a family man ready for a casual outing with his wife and child.

She wondered if Mrs. Strong would be able to provide any helpful information that would speed his investigation.

"Do you have sunscreen?" Josh asked when Michelle sat at the table with her toast and tea a few minutes later.

"Yes, why?"

"We'll all need it today. I'm renting a convertible for the trip."

Michelle looked at him. "Why?"

"Why not? Don't you think that'd be fun? It's a beautiful day, not as hot as it was earlier in the week, and I think it would be more fun to drive with the top down and really be able to see things. Fun for Penny, too."

"I think it would be fantastic! I've always wanted to ride in one."

"Then today is your lucky day!"

Josh and Penny left right after breakfast to pick up the rental car. Michelle straightened up the house while she waited. Hurriedly dusting and vacuuming the main floor, she was surprised at the sense of belonging. Granted, Abby and her friends had skillfully mingled her furnishings with Josh's so she felt a bit more at home. But this was something more.

As she picked up Penny's toys, she felt a sense of connection. Was this what being part of a close family was like ? She liked it.

Glancing at her watch, she wondered if she had time to start a load of laundry. It must have piled up over the week and she needed to get a start if she wanted everything done before the next work week started since they were taking today to go to Baton Rouge.

Gathering Penny's clothes, Michelle then headed for Josh's room. She hadn't been in it since she moved her things out last Sunday. Pausing in the doorway, she caught her breath. His scent filled her senses. Slowly she studied the room, seeing Josh's stamp everywhere, from the tumble of keys and change on his dresser, to the carelessly tossed socks and jeans near, but not quite in, the hamper. His bed was rumpled. Didn't he make it each morning?

They all shared the hall bathroom and he was pretty neat there—hanging up his towel and clearing away his shaving things. But he obviously felt free to do what he pleased in his own room.

Which was as it should be, Michelle thought as she gathered the clothes.

Josh and Penny arrived in a bright red convertible a few minutes later. Penny called Michelle from the car, standing up in the front seat.

"Come and see!" she squealed when Michelle appeared at the front door.

Jumping up and down she raised her hands over her head. "No roof, Michelle, no roof!"

"Easy, squirt. Don't go tumbling out." Josh reached for her shirt, to keep her from losing her balance.

"I see—no roof." Michelle laughed at the child's enthusiasm.

She was a lucky little girl to have an indulgent father. Michelle's grandmother would never have tolerated such behavior. Yet why shouldn't a child share her exuberance?

"Ready?" Josh called.

"Just a second." Michelle closed up and hurried down the sidewalk to the dashing car.

"Jump over the side, Michelle," Penny instructed.

"I think I better open the door first, honey."

"Daddy dropped me over the side and jumped in that way."

Eyeing Josh's wide grin, Michelle laughed in sheer happiness. "I just bet he did. This time, though, I better get in the normal way."

"Chicken," Josh said, teasing her.

"I beg your pardon."

"Live a little. Slide in over the side. Why have a convertible if you can't be bold?"

Bold? He could write the book on bold, she thought, biting her lip in indecision. Scenes from movies flashed through her mind, hands on the side, jumping in.

"Just plant that luscious bottom on the side and lean back. We'll catch you," Josh instructed, laughing at her.

"We'll catch you, Michelle. Do it!" Penny shouted.

Tossing her purse into the backseat, Michelle did just that. Tumbling into the seat amid laughter, she felt exhilarated and free. Josh and Penny were squished when she lost her balance, legs still over the side of the door, and fell sprawled almost the width of the seat. But no one minded. Everyone laughed

Straightening, Michelle giggled, wanting to throw her arms around Josh and thank him for all the ways he was changing her life. She cherished the hours she spent with him.

"Good idea, huh?" Josh asked as he settled Penny in her car seat in the back.

"Great idea. Is this how you do all your investigations?" Michelle asked as she fastened her seat belt. For the first time she felt like a different woman, one who was interesting and exciting—no longer quiet and shy.

"Not usually. But then this isn't a normal investigation."

"True. I'm ready."

"Then we're off."

The ride passed swiftly. Josh began with telling Penny stories. When he ran out, they all sang songs. Michelle was amazed at the lyrics she remembered from when she'd been a child. They arrived in Baton Rouge almost before they knew it.

Michelle directed Josh to the nursing home.

"I can drop you and Penny somewhere if you like. There must be a park around somewhere," Josh said as he entered the drive for the residential facility.

"I want to see Mrs. Strong again. I bet she'd love to see Penny. She's not ill, she just can't do everything for herself anymore. She's confined to a wheelchair, but I know she'd love to see a little girl running around. And I want to hear what she has to say. Caroline and Brandon spoke with her before. I only met her when they renewed their vows."

They met with Edith Strong on the terrace of the retirement home. While the temperature was high, there was a slight breeze and sitting in the shade proved comfortable.

As Michelle predicted, Edith was delighted to have them visit. When Penny expressed curiosity about her wheelchair, she invited her into her lap and gave her a ride around the terrace.

"Another vehicle with no roof," Josh said softly to Michelle as they watched the two enjoying themselves.

"I told you Mrs. Strong would like Penny. And from the look on the faces of some of the other residents, I bet they all are delighted to have her here."

A few minutes later, Josh began his questions. Michelle was surprised at all Mrs. Strong remembered, and how much she knew about her family.

At one point, the older woman looked at her as if

picking up on that surprise. "Your grandmother and I were best friends before she interfered in your mother's life. I disapproved and our friendship cooled. But there's no truth to the rumor that elderly people forget things. I'm as sharp as I ever was. As was Eugenia, until the end, right?"

Michelle nodded, intrigued by the glimpses of her own life when she was a baby. Caroline had said their father loved their mother, but it seemed more real when Edith Strong talked about their obvious love for each other.

The old sense of loss rose when she heard again how her grandmother had manipulated her daughter's life in such a cruel fashion. Had Eugenia Talmadge not interfered, Michelle's life might have been vastly different.

As they walked back to the car an hour later, Michelle's desire to find her father was strengthened. She wanted to know what he'd done with his life over the years. To discover if he was in need, or had moved on and made a new life for himself.

Josh lifted Penny over the side of the red car and set her on the car seat, then opened the door for Michelle.

"You okay, babe?"

She nodded. "I will be once you find my father. It's so sad, isn't it. They were so in love and to be separated like that. You know, my sisters and I have a theory that when our mother got sick, she just gave up. I wonder what would have happened if she hadn't died. Do you think she would have gone looking for him?"

"Yes."

She stared at him hopefully. "Really?"

"Sure. You had to get your determination and

perseverance from someone, probably your mother. If she'd lived, I bet she'd have discovered the deception your grandmother initiated and tracked down Sam to tell him everything."

Michelle smiled, the ache in her heart easing a bit. "Thanks, Josh. I don't know that for sure but it's nice to hear."

He placed a finger beneath her chin and raised her face, lowering his until Michelle could feel the puff of his breath against her cheeks. "Honey, I'm sorry today's been tough. But we have some new clues. I'll find your father."

Nodding, Michelle couldn't move.

Mesmerized by the look in his eyes, she remembered his blunt statement on the riverbank last weekend. Heat seeped into her, hotter than that from the sun. Why was being around this man enough to melt any common sense she possessed?

"And if you keep looking at me like that, I'll move it to the number one priority at the agency."

He brushed his lips across hers and then straightened.

"Wanna go for a ride!" Penny said impatiently.

"Okay, miss bossy," Josh said with a laugh. Let's go eat lunch and then Michelle can show us the old family homestead."

"You want to see Talmadge Hall?" she asked in surprise. "Why? Do you think you can find some clue my father left, like an old letter in the crack of a tree?"

He grinned as he made sure Penny was fastened in securely. "Nope, just want to see where you were raised." His gaze met hers. "Any problem with that?"

Secretly pleased, Michelle shook her head. She hadn't missed Talmadge Hall a single day since she left. But if Josh wanted to see it, she didn't mind.

Sated from lunch, they were all quiet as Josh drove down the wide drive that led to the antebellum home. The yard was kept up. Rosalee came by once a week to keep an eye on things. It was for sale, but taking a long time to sell.

The place had an air of desertion surrounding it, she noted, as he drove down the long driveway. The trees on either side were in full leaf, the Spanish moss heavy. There were dead leaves on the veranda, and a branch or two that had obviously fallen during a recent rainstorm. No one had lived in the house since they'd put it up for sale. It'd probably be another few days before the grounds keepers were back for the biweekly lawn mowing.

Taking her keys, Michelle let them into the old mansion. It smelled musty and stale. The place had been listed for sale for a couple of months, but Caroline said there'd been little interest.

"No wonder you don't like my car, if this is where you were raised," Josh said slowly, taking in the crystal chandelier, the fine furnishings and expensive paintings.

Michelle turned swiftly and crossed the entry to stand deliberately in front of him. "I might have judged your car hastily, Josh. Don't make the same mistake about this house. It was a shrine for Eugenia Talmadge, but not a place to call home by her granddaughters."

He put his big hands on her shoulders and drew her closer.

"Let's shock your grandmother's ghost," he said

whimsically.

Chapter Seven

Michelle felt a shiver of anticipation. She took a deep breath. "What did you have in mind?" She didn't trust that gleam in Josh's eye.

He smiled and shrugged, his hands tightening slightly on her shoulders. "What would shock her the most, dancing barefoot in the entry, playing tag on the ground floor, or sliding down the banister?"

Michelle laughed, trying to ignore the twinge of disappointment. What had she expected him to say?

"All of the above! And I especially wished to slide down the banister when I was a child," she confided.

"Can we go?" Penny asked.

Josh released his hold as the adults looked at her. "Go where?" Josh asked.

"Home."

"In a bit. We want to see Michelle's house."

Penny's eyes widened. "This is Michelle's house?"

"It used to be, when I was a little girl like you," Michelle said. "Want to see my bedroom?"

"You gots toys?"

"Have, not gots. There aren't any toys left. We're trying

to sell the house and all the personal things have been taken away. But you can see my bed and where I used to play. And I'll show you Auntie Abby's and Auntie Caroline's rooms, too."

"'Kay."

"Come on, then." Michelle reached out her hand and was pleased when Penny trustingly placed hers in it. They climbed the long stairway to the spacious second story. Walking down the hall toward her old bedroom, Michelle was assailed with memories. Many happy ones of her and her sisters running between their rooms, telling secrets and laughing. But the echo of their grandmother's stern voice sounded. She'd never evidenced any joy and seemed determined to squelch any signs in her granddaughters as well.

"This is it." Michelle stepped inside and glanced around. It was a lovely room. The windows were tall with one set of French doors opening to the wrap around veranda on the second floor. But it looked cold and lonely.

Penny raced to the French doors and gazed outside, then walked around, touching things until she came to the canopy bed. Looking at the canopy, she smiled.

"Can I get up?" she asked.

Michelle crossed to lift the child into the bed. Penny promptly lay back and eyed the lacy confection above her head. "Like a little house," she said.

"I liked that bed when I was little. When I was a teenager, I wished for the kind of bed where side curtains could drop down as well. That would have cocooned me from the rest of the family."

Josh leaned against the door jamb, watching. Folding his arms across his chest, he studied the room. "I believe this room is larger than the first floor of my house."

Michelle looked over at him in surprise. Then she frowned. "Don't get any ideas, Josh. This is all show. And the price for it was steep. My grandmother was obsessed with the Talmadge family and Talmadge Hall. She mortgaged it to the hilt. If we ever get it sold, we'll be lucky to get enough to pay all the debts. And you already know what she did to my parents—all in the name of family prestige."

"Still must be a come-down to be living in my place now."

"Not a bit. There's warmth and a feeling of love in your home. You're giving Penny something money can't buy, a feeling of being wanted and cherished. I'd have given anything to have had that as a child."

Flushing with the intensity of her words, Michelle turned and wandered to the windows. She'd been lucky with her sisters. They'd forged a bond that enabled them to endure the loss of their parents and the lack of warmth and love in the huge old family home. At least she'd had that.

"Where's Auntie Abby's room?" Penny asked, sliding down from the bed.

"This way." Michelle started from the room, stopping when she reached the door. Josh was blocking the way. And from the look on his face, he wasn't planning to move any time soon.

"Want to see Abby's room, too?" she asked.

"I think I'd like to hear a bit more about Michelle's childhood," he said slowly.

"That was a long time ago."

"Not so long ago. Was it so bad?"

"Maybe not so bad. Especially when we were little like Penny. I don't think grandmother wanted to be bothered by little kids, so we had a series of nannies who watched us. We had a lot more freedom then than when we reached our teens. It was then that we started eating meals with grandmother and learning proper behavior. With the intent of attracting the right man and making an advantageous alliance," she ended bitterly.

"Advantageous alliance?"

She smiled wryly. "Her term for marriage."

"I want to see Auntie Abby's room, Daddy," Penny said, squeezing between him and the door frame.

"Let it go, Josh. It was a long time ago. I left as soon as I graduated from high school and only came back once in a while when I couldn't get out of it."

Josh moved out into the hall. "We can discuss this at another time."

Leading the way across the hall to Abby's old room, Michelle wondered why he kept on.

"Of course, your investigative instincts."

"What investigative instincts?"

"That's why you want to know more, it's part of some ingrained work ethic because of your job."

Josh didn't respond as he watched Michelle show Abby's room to his daughter.

Wanting to know more about her childhood had nothing to do with being an investigator, he realized. He plain wanted to know more about Michelle. What made her laugh or cry. What she'd loved as a child. How she had coped without a mother and father all the times when parents are so important. Had her grandmother gone to school events? Had she ever held them, rocked them. Maybe when young.

But from what she'd said, maybe no. He was grateful she had happy memories of the nannies who had cared for her.

He looked around the lavish old home. She'd grown up in luxury. It didn't matter that her grandmother had gone into debt toward the end, Michelle had still been raised with extravagances he could only imagine.

And would never have.

It was a good thing their alliance was temporary. He could never offer her a home like this.

And sooner or later, she'd want more than he could afford.

Hadn't that been one of Sylvia's complaints? She'd wanted him to kill himself slaving away at some high powered law firm, racking up billable hours so money would pour in. And still be available for all the social events she wanted to attend.

Yet being an investigator was something he loved. He couldn't imagine making a living doing anything else. And, of course, his job was the sole reason Michelle had come into his life—even for a short time.

They explored the second floor until they'd seen into

every room. Michelle even led them briefly to the attic to show Josh where Caroline and Brandon had found the boxes that also led to their discovery about her father. He listened to all she had to say, trying to get a feeling for things unsaid.

As they headed back downstairs, Josh scooped Penny up and paused at the head of the stairs.

"This is your chance, Michelle. Go for it."

"What are you talking about?"

"Sliding down the banister."

He found life more fun when trying new things and daring to take chances. Would Michelle feel the same?

She looked at the long expanse of highly polished mahogany, at the steep drop to the side and shook her head.

"Of course if you are some sissy, chicken girl, I guess you can't do it," he teased.

"I'm likely to fall off and break my neck! There was a good reason grandmother forbid us to even try."

He grinned, and started down the stairs. He'd give her one minute. He could recognize indecision mixed with raw desire when he saw it.

"I'll stand beneath the railing and catch you if you fall. You'll probably never have another chance," he called over his shoulder.

Michelle watched as he went down the stairs, but she made no move to take the stairs.

Josh set Penny on the marble floor and pointed to the doorway into the living room.

"Wait there," he said in a stage whisper, "and watch Michelle."

Walking to stand beneath the highest part of the stairs, he looked up.

He could see her take a breath and the smile of pure delight that spread.

"Catch me at the bottom," she instructed, as she sat sideways on the wood.

Josh had no sooner moved to the base of the stairs than she let go a shriek and came sailing down the railing, plunging right into him. She was laughing as they tangled and fell back to the floor. He was glad he'd been there. She'd had no control and could have hurt herself.

Penny laughed and ran across to kneel beside them. "I want to do that, Daddy. That's fun!"

Josh slowly sat up, Michelle still in his arms. Her laughter was infectious and he began to chuckle. "Not this time, Penny. You can't reach the banister like Michelle can. Maybe when you're older."

"That was wonderful. I felt like I was flying." Michelle exclaimed, still laughing.

"I want to fly, Daddy!" Penny insisted.

Michelle jumped up and reached down a hand for Josh. "Okay, punkin, we'll see what we can do, right Daddy?"

Josh didn't release her hand when he rose, but pulled her closer. "Just how do you propose to do that?"

"She could do it for just a few feet. I'll put her on it and hold her, you catch her at the bottom. It was so much fun I wished I had been able to do it when I was younger. Let's indulge her."

As you were not indulged, Josh thought, nodding in agreement. "Okay, but only for a few feet."

Penny loved sliding and insisted on playing that new game a dozen times more. Josh finally put his foot down, asking Michelle if she wanted another try.

She shook her head.

"No. That was great. But once was special. To do it again might not be as special. I want to always remember it as it was."

She sat on the top step and began to take off her shoes. "But I'll take you up on your other offer."

He nodded and toed off his shoes. But there was another way he wished they could shock her grandmother's ghost, and it had nothing to do with dancing or playing tag.

She rose and shyly looked at him.

He was beginning to understand this complex woman who was his wife. His temporary wife. And that worried him.

"May I have this dance?" he asked with a mock bow.

Penny stood on the bottom step and clapped her hands. "Dance!"

"With Michelle the first time, okay?"

"Then me."

"Then you."

Penny sat on the stairs and took off her shoes, watching them dance and calling out to them to hurry.

Josh swept Michelle into his arms and swooped and turned and carried them all around the wide foyer. The marble was cool beneath their feet, the humid Mississippi air wafted in from the opened front door. Before long they were both hot and breathless.

Josh stopped and kissed her. She was warm and smelled

heavenly. The taste of her lips was sweet as honey and he wanted her as he hadn't wanted a woman in years. Maybe never.

"My turn," Penny said, racing across the foyer.

Josh pulled back, his eyes finding Michelle's. The heat in her cheeks was not all due to their exertion. He recognized the dazed look in her eyes and something grew inside. He didn't need Michelle to tell him that she wasn't very experienced. He had only to look into her eyes to see the signs.

"Okay." Josh reached down to pick up Penny. He didn't relinquish Michelle's hand even when she tugged.

"We can all three dance," he said.

When he saw the delight in her eyes, he was glad he'd suggested it.

They danced around and around, Penny shrieking with laughter. Michelle giggling at them all.

Finally, Josh stopped.

"Enough! It's hot as blazes in here."

He put Penny down and straightened, arching his back and raising his arms over his head to ease some of his muscles. Penny wasn't growing any lighter as she grew up.

Michelle laughed and reached out to touch his shoulder.

"Tag—you're it! Run, Penny, don't let Daddy get you."

With that, Michelle took off toward the dining room, her bare feet slapping against the floor. Penny was only a step or two behind her.

Josh hesitated a moment before taking off after them. He glanced around.

"I hope you can see this, Eugenia Talmadge. This is

what a home is supposed to be like, full of laughter and fun and children running. The things that make happy memories."

When they at last headed back to New Orleans, Penny quickly fell asleep in her car seat. Michelle was feeling a bit tired herself, but didn't want to miss a single moment of the day. She never would have imaged the fun that awaited when they left home that morning. She wondered if she'd ever spend such a marvelous day again.

And it was all because of Josh.

"You said you got some more clues from Mrs. Strong?" she asked, remembering the real reason for the trip.

"A few more—enough to open a couple of other avenues of inquiry, at least. We'll see where it leads. This takes time."

"I know. And it's not like there's any rush. Caroline found out months ago. After more than twenty years, I can't expect him to be easy to find. Especially if he thought the law was after him. He could have changed his name, couldn't he?"

"Yes, and that'd make it more difficult. But it's still early, give me some time." Josh glanced at her. "You're not regretting your bargain, are you? Is Penny proving a problem?"

"What? Oh, you mean our marriage? No, I'm not sorry we did that. I'm glad I can provide the day care for her. And she's getting better around me. Look at today. In another few weeks, we'll be best friends."

"Just don't get so close you break her heart when you leave."

Michelle nodded. For a while today she'd forgotten she was only a temporary part of their family. Laughing and playing with Penny and Josh had been so much fun it was hard to imagine she might not have many days like this. Once Josh discovered where her father was, his side of the agreement would be fulfilled. And once Caroline had her baby and Penny was eligible for after-school care, Michelle would no longer be needed. She'd be on her own again.

Josh was right to warn her not to get too involved. Penny wasn't the only one who could have her heart broken.

Keeping the business nature of their relationship in the forefront of her mind, Michelle tried to build some reserve into her dealings with Josh and Penny. Sunday she declined their offer to join them at the park, pleading the need to do laundry, grocery shopping and maybe even get to some of the work Josh had brought home on Friday night.

But she couldn't help feeling left out when they departed.

Knowing she could have gone didn't ease the sensation, but working around the small house helped. She took pride in caring for Josh's things. When the house was spotless, the laundry put away and the grocery list made, she sat down for a few moments' rest before heading out to the store.

Impulsively, she dialed Abby's number. Her sister answered on the second ring.

"What's up?" she asked seeing it was Michelle calling.

"Not much. Josh took Penny to the park and I'm going shopping soon. I wanted to thank you and your friends for moving my things. Everything looked perfect when we got here."

"So you said on the message you left last Monday. Sorry I missed your call. Work is frantic. But in a few weeks I'm due for some vacation and can I use it!"

"Your ER training program will be over by then?"

"Yes. So the timing's perfect. I'll take my vacation and then request a permanent assignment to the emergency room when I return. If St. Joe can't do it, I might put out feelers to some of the other hospitals. I really want to do this type of nursing. How's my favorite niece?"

Michelle smiled. "She's your only one so far and only by marriage."

"If Caroline has a boy, she'll still be my only one— and favorite."

"Don't get too attached," Michelle said.

"Why not?"

Oops. "Well, if Caroline has a girl, you might want to make her your favorite."

"If that happens, I won't have favorites. I wish she and Brandon would agree to find out the baby's gender ahead of time."

"I like it that we won't know until the baby's born."

They chatted for a few minutes. When she hung up, Michelle felt better. She'd always have her sisters, even when her marriage ended. And there was nothing saying she and Abby and Caroline couldn't continue to see Penny from time to time.

Of course that'd mean seeing Josh, too. Which wouldn't be all bad, she thought as she headed out to shop.

Since the Fourth of July holiday had the garages closed

Monday, Michelle's car was still in the shop Tuesday. Josh drove her and Penny in, stopping in to see the child care facilities which Penny proudly showed off.

Michelle almost asked him to stop by her office so she could show *him* off.

She caught herself before she asked. Where was the distance she was trying to put between them?

Her car was repaired by the end of the day and Josh arranged to have it delivered to the office. She was touched by his thoughtful gesture, but she secretly wished he'd picked them up.

Wednesday he didn't call her at the office as had been his habit the previous week. Michelle missed the calls, but had only herself to blame. She kept telling herself she wanted some distance between them, so she shouldn't complain that it was working.

Thursday afternoon Josh called Michelle at work.

"Is something wrong?" she asked. Last week he'd called before lunch each day. This week, he'd been too busy. Or at least that's what he'd told her last night when she mentioned it at dinner.

"One of my operatives is sick. We've been working on a suspected insurance fraud for your firm. Which includes someone watching him around the clock. Since Mel's sick, I'll need to take the night surveillance. Can you manage all right at home alone?"

"Sure. This is one of the reasons you married me, remember, so I can be there for Penny when something like this happens. No problem. We get along fine. Will you be home at all tonight?"

"Probably not. I'll swing by the house in a few minutes and pick up a few things—something to read and some soft drinks to keep me going. Tomorrow I'll be able to pull rank and assign someone else, but this caught me by surprise."

"No problem. This isn't dangerous, is it?"

"No. The man swears he injured his back and can hardly walk. The doctors can find no evidence of trauma, but there's the possibility he's telling the truth. Pain can be a tricky thing. That's what we're hoping to find out. No danger."

"Okay, then I'll see you tomorrow after work, I guess."

Michelle treated Penny to dinner at one of her favorite fast food places—the one where there was play equipment. Penny entertained herself for an hour on all the climbing gear and bouncing balls.

The house was silent when Michelle let them in. She quickly got Penny ready for bed, read her a long story, and tucked her in for the night. Then she wandered into the living room. There were no new folders or stacks of papers. Josh had obviously not brought any work home for her.

His new temporary help was proving adaptable and able to keep up with the day-to-day routine. And the backlog was almost caught up, he'd told her Tuesday.

She switched on the television, aware of how much she missed Josh.

"Oh my gosh, he's not home one night and I feel at loose ends. What happens when the marriage ends?"

Michelle asked herself as she flipped through the different channels.

Nothing appealed. She switched it off.

Her phone rang.

Caroline was on the other end.

"Hi, how's married life?" her sister asked.

"Great," Michelle forced enthusiasm into her tone.

"I still feel badly y'all haven't had a honeymoon. So Brandon and I want to watch Penny this weekend. Give you and Josh another night alone. I know you adore Penny, but you two newlyweds need some time just the two of you."

She and Josh alone in the house?

Michelle's imagination kicked in and she smiled at the thought. Maybe they could dance barefoot like they had in Baton Rouge. The memory of his kiss at Talmadge Hall surfaced. That she'd like even better. Frowning when she realized where her thoughts were leading, she shook her head.

"I don't know. She can be fairly rambunctious."

"We loved having her before. She's a delight. Besides, Brandon and I both will be here and it'll be good practice for us. We'll have one of our own in a few months, remember?"

"And you need to rest!"

"Phooey, I'm feeling great. I had a checkup earlier this week and everything looks perfect. Come on, let Penny come visit. You and Josh deserve some time alone. You only get to be newlyweds once."

"I'll check with him and let you know."

"I'll hold. Ask him now so we'll know for sure."

"Actually, he's out on a stakeout tonight," Michelle said

slowly. "He won't be home until tomorrow. I don't want to call him in case he doesn't want to give his location away."

"Then ask tomorrow and let us know. You two could go out to dinner and dancing and then return home and be alone all weekend."

"I'll check and let you know. Thanks, Caroline, this is really great."

Michelle continued to feel like a fraud and wondered if Caroline could detect it in her tone.

The last thing she wanted was to be alone with Josh. Wasn't she trying to keep a distance between them to guard her heart?

Guard her heart?

Was she falling in love with the man?

No!

He was searching for her father and she was a temporary mother for Penny. There was nothing more involved.

"Tell me what the doctor said," Michelle said in an effort to escape her tumultuous thoughts.

She envied Caroline's happiness and assurance of her husband's love. Would Michelle ever find a strong love to carry her through eternity?

After talking with Caroline, Michelle felt more restless than before. She decided to take a long soak in the tub to settle down for bed. She had the house to herself and nothing pressing to do.

Checking on Penny before running the water, she felt her heart melt a bit more at the sight of the enchanting little girl. Kissing her softly on her cheek, Michelle felt a wealth of love well up.

She wished she could stay around to see Penny grow. When would she give up her teddy bear? Would she ever give up her baseball cap or stop saying gots? How would she like kindergarten in the fall? She played well with the other children in day care, and already had made friends.

Michelle envied her that. Shyness was such an awkward trait.

Feeling indulgent, Michelle dumped in fragrant bath salts when she ran the water for her bath. She found a bunch of candles and lit a dozen, enjoying the soft glow of candlelight as she slipped into the silken hot water. Leaning back, she closed her eyes, letting her thoughts drift as she relaxed.

She'd enjoy the hot bath until the water grew cold, then go to bed and start that new book she'd bought. She'd left the door open, though Penny usually slept through the night. But she was in charge with Josh gone and didn't want to take any chances the little girl would wake up and be scared if Michelle didn't hear her call immediately.

The water soothed, its warmth seeping into her, relaxing her. If she began to feel sleepy, she'd have to get out, but until then, it was nice to just drift.

"I wondered what was causing the flickering light," Josh said from the doorway.

Michelle sat straight up in startled shock.

"What are you doing here?" she cried. Snatching the washrag, she held it in front of her. It wasn't big enough. Heat seeped through her that had nothing to do with the water.

"I live here," he said with amusement.

"I thought you were going to be gone all night."

She was conscious of his gaze moving across her. Shifting the washcloth, she tried to vainly cover more of her bare skin.

"And this is how you indulge yourself when I'm gone?" he said, a slow smile lighting his face as he let his gaze trail over her.

"Get out, Josh."

"I'm not really in, just standing here in the doorway."

"Close the door—with you on the outside," she snapped, feeling twice as hot under his eyes.

Why hadn't she used bubble bath so she could sink beneath the bubbles and at least maintain a modicum of modesty? Or closed the door and taken the chance Penny wouldn't wake?

Or just take a quick shower for all that?

Instead of doing as she ordered, Josh stepped into the dimly lit room. Squatting beside the tub, he leaned over and kissed her soft lips.

"You are so beautiful," he said softly, kissing her again.

Despite common sense arguing against it, Michelle reached up one hand to his neck and held on while Josh deepened the kiss.

"You shouldn't be here," she whispered a minute later when he pulled back and gazed into her eyes. Her heart raced. She could scarcely breathe.

"I told you, I live here."

"What happened to the stakeout?"

He laughed and stood up. "The guy blew it. Some friend drove up in this fancy car and the man just about did a jig looking it over. I have almost an entire roll of film showing him with no apparent impediment to normal living. More than enough for the insurance company. So I came home. I didn't notice that you left the door open when you bathed before."

"I did it to hear Penny if she woke. Would you please let me have a bit of privacy so I can get out and dressed?"

He shrugged. "If you insist."

"I do!"

He sauntered to the door, and glanced over his shoulder. "I could help," he said audaciously.

"Get out!"

Laughing, Josh complied, pulling the door shut behind him.

"Come and sit with me while I eat," he called.

Michelle wanted to sink beneath the water and hide, but knew that was a vain thought. She couldn't stay in the bathroom forever.

But relaxation was a lost hope. She felt tight as a drawn bowstring.

Rising quickly, she dried off and donned her light gown and robe. Blowing out the candles, she brushed her hair and debated what to do. She had to face the man sometime. Might as well get it over with. Taking a deep breath, she headed reluctantly for the kitchen.

She refused to be embarrassed. They were married. He'd been married before and had seen it all, she was sure. Yet she couldn't help feel flustered when she stepped inside and Josh turned and smiled wickedly at her.

"Next time, maybe I'll join you."

Chapter Eight

Michelle ignored the suggestive comment and crossed to the refrigerator. If she could hide her embarrassment, maybe he wouldn't tease her.

"Shall I make you something hot to eat or would a sandwich and salad do?"

"Anything. I got a burger late this afternoon, but I'm hungry now. How did it go with Penny?"

"Fine."

She quickly prepared him a roast beef sandwich, and tossed a small green salad. Setting both before him at the small breakfast table, she returned to the counter to put away the food.

"Stop fussing and come sit with me," Josh said around a mouthful of sandwich.

Michelle looked at him, drawn like a moth to the flame. She loved being with him, enjoyed hearing him talk. Found his way of thinking fascinating. She'd never spent so much time with a man before. She liked it.

She pulled out a chair and sat. Not too close, but near enough she could reach out and touch him if she dared.

"Tell me about the case. Did the man know you saw him? Did you get enough proof?"

"He never knew I was there. I need to make sure the prints come out clearly before confronting him. But I'm sure the scam will end tomorrow. This will save the insurance company a ton of money."

"Which means a healthy fee for you, right?"

"Healthy enough."

He took another bite of the sandwich. "This is good, but you look good enough to eat," he said with a grin.

Flustered, Michelle sought to change the topic. "Caroline called tonight. She and Brandon offered to watch Penny this weekend."

"Why?"

Michelle hesitated. This topic could lead back to the one she'd been trying to avoid.

"Actually, she said it was to get some practice. For when her baby comes."

Josh bit into the sandwich again and studied her. "There's more."

She wrinkled her nose. "No wonder you're good at your job. You never take anything at face value. Actually," Michelle hesitated, then rushed into speech, "she thought it would give us a weekend alone. To go to dinner or something."

Slowly his eyes lit up. Then he smiled.

Michelle didn't trust that smile.

"What?" she blurted out.

"I think Caroline's offer is brilliant. I'm sure Penny will love visiting them. Tell them I appreciate the offer."

"We don't have to go out to dinner, that was just an idea."

"And a good one. Dinner and dancing. Though not with bare feet like at Talmadge Hall, maybe." Josh finished his sandwich. "And with Penny gone, we don't have to worry about making noise in the night, or getting up early. We could sleep in as long as we wanted."

"Making noise in the night?"

Josh leaned over and drew Michelle from her chair, into his lap. His hands held her loosely, but Michelle suspected that if she made a move to leave, he'd clamp down.

His gaze caught hers and he leaned closer. "Sometimes when people make love they make noise. Have you thought about what I asked on our wedding day?"

Michelle blinked mesmerized by the hot longing clearly evident in Josh's gaze. The wash of desire that swept through surprised her. She wanted to say yes, but her innate caution held her back.

"I still don't think it's a good idea to get involved that way."

"Aren't you tempted the least little bit?"

She sighed and leaned against him. "I never stop thinking about it," she confessed.

"Me, too," he said and kissed her, his mouth capturing hers in a manner designed to drive her out of her mind. Her heart kicked in double time and the world seemed to spin out of control.

"Josh, stop!" She pushed back and stood up, breathing hard. Staring at him Michelle knew she'd like nothing more than to fling herself into his arms and never have him stop kissing her.

But was she ready for a fling? Didn't she want more than just physical pleasure? She wanted caring and affection. Love.

"Now what?" he asked, leaning back in his chair and tucking his fingers in the pockets of his trousers. His expression was impassive, giving nothing away.

She tried to gather her thoughts. "Nothing's changed. We agreed to marry so you'd look for my father while I provide child care for Penny. Now you want to change the rules. That's not fair."

"It's perfectly fair if we both agree. You just said you never stop thinking about it."

"But that doesn't mean I want to...to give into..."

Josh came to his feet. "Say what you mean, Michelle."

She shook her head. She wasn't sure she knew what she meant. Maybe it would be better if he thought she was rejecting him. She only had so much willpower and he tested it every time he came near her.

"I get the picture," he said coolly. "I won't trouble you again."

With that he strode from the room.

Michelle watched him leave, heard his steps on the stairs.

"Great job, Michelle. Now you've really done it."

Slowly she took his plates to the sink and rinsed them. How could she tell him the truth? He'd suspect she was angling for just what she was trying to avoid. Yet she hated him thinking she didn't want him.

Still they had no future together. Hadn't he made it clear he wasn't interested in a permanent relationship again? She wasn't sure what had happened in his first marriage, but whatever it had been sure made him wary around women. It had taken him two days after she made her outlandish offer before he could bring himself to accept—and she knew he'd only done so for Penny.

Nothing had changed.

Sighing softly, she turned off the light and went up to bed. But sleep was a long time coming.

Caroline called Michelle at work on Friday morning.

"Hi, I won't talk long, just wondered if you've spoken with Josh yet?"

"Yes. He said he appreciated the invitation. I meant to call you back. Sorry, I got busy," Michelle said slowly.

"No problem. We thought we'd stop by today and pick her up. That'll give you an extra night. And you could sleep in late two mornings in a row. I bet that sounds like heaven, right?"

Michelle gripped the receiver. Great, she'd have two nights with Josh's cool and distant attitude instead of one and with no Penny there to act as a buffer. Yet she couldn't say anything to Caroline without worrying her.

"Are you sure this won't be too much for you? I thought you were supposed to take things easy?"

"Don't be a worrywart. I'm fine. And Penny's a doll. We plan to go to the park and then rent some Disney videos and make popcorn. She'll have a ball."

"Ummm." Lucky Penny.

"Something wrong?"

"Nothing!" Michelle answered immediately. "When did

you want her to be ready?" She saw no way to avoid the visit. No way to avoid being alone with Josh for two whole days.

"We'll stop by at six. That'll give you time to get home and pack a few things for her, won't it?"

"Yes. That'll work well. See you then."

As she hung up the phone, Michelle wondered if she could insist Penny return early Sunday morning.

No, that would defeat Caroline's gesture.

Sighing, she was beginning to wish she'd never gotten into such a tangle. She wanted to know about her father, but wondered if the price was going to prove too high.

That evening after Penny left with Caroline and Brandon, Michelle busied herself preparing the grill she'd found in Josh's garage. She'd much rather barbecue outside than be confined in the small kitchen alone with Josh. Especially after last night.

She had the coals glowing and a fruit salad prepared when he came home. He had a stack of folders in a large case. Obviously he, too, planned to keep things businesslike.

Michelle explained that Penny had already left and would be home sometime Sunday afternoon. Josh nodded and headed for the living room, asking her to call him when dinner was ready.

Perversely, she missed the companionship they'd shared during the past two weeks while she prepared dinner. She'd deliberately set up dinner just this way, and now regretted it.

She missed Penny's chatter as well. It was lonely and quiet in the back yard with only herself for company.

"Better get used to it, girl," she muttered as she rotated

the chicken on the grill. As soon as their mock marriage ended, she'd be alone again.

Michelle wondered if she would ever find anyone to love, to build a life with.

Someone with a quick mind, a bit unconventional, who could kiss like every fantasy ever invented.

Someone like Josh.

Ruthlessly squelching her thoughts, she speared a drumstick, and lifted it to the platter. Time to eat and stop thinking.

Not thinking was easier said than done, Michelle admitted later that evening.

Dinner had been quick and impersonal. Josh ate, left the table and resumed the work he'd brought home. It didn't take long to clean the plates.

Then Michelle was at a loose end.

In the past she might have called a friend or one of her sisters, but anyone she called tonight would find it extremely odd that a newly wed woman didn't want to spend special alone time with her husband.

Maybe she shouldn't have conspired to keep the truth of the situation from her sisters. It was hard to carry the burden alone.

Not quite alone. Josh shared it with her.

Drying her hands, Michelle headed for the living room. She'd offer to help him with the office work. She'd done quite a bit over the last couple of weeks and knew exactly what he expected.

He looked up when she stepped into the room, a look of inquiry on his face.

"I thought I could help," she said, feeling flustered again. When would she be beyond that. Granted he was a good looking man. But she'd seen good looking men before and didn't feel this way.

"This is the last of the backlog. If I can get caught up by the end of the weekend, then things will be back to normal at the office. I offered the temp a permanent job today. She's going to let me know on Monday. If she stays, I'll bring her up to speed with the rest of the procedures. So far she's a hard worker and keeps up with the day-to-day load."

"Good."

Michelle took a folder and began to read.

Except for the odd tension that seemed to hum between them, the evening was not very different from others they'd shared. Josh worked diligently through the files, scanning reports, checking the billing records, and jotting notes on a sheet of paper where he wanted to do further follow-up.

Michelle looked up to watch him every time she finished with a folder. He looked tired. Her heart lurched. Was he working too hard?

She knew that, despite the work of his two operatives, things had fallen behind when he'd had the difficulty with Penny's day care, but surely things were getting better there now.

"Why don't you go up to bed, Josh," she said when the clock chimed ten. "You look tired."

He shrugged, but didn't raise his gaze from the folder on his lap.

"You have all day tomorrow to work on these folders."

"No, I have an assignment tomorrow."

"Oh." So much for Caroline's brilliant idea of giving them time together.

He looked up. After a minute, he said, "Want to go with me?"

Michelle didn't hesitate. "I'd love to. Are you going undercover?"

"You've been watching too many TV detective shows. There's rarely a need to go undercover in my line of work."

"Okay, so what are you doing tomorrow?"

"Watching a place in the Quarter to see if we can spot who's been passing counterfeit bills."

"Isn't that something the cops would do?"

"They have a stakeout, but the owner suspects a member of his extended family and if he can discover who's doing it before the cops, he might be able to minimize the fallout."

Michelle gazed off into space, envisioning her and Josh on a case together. Smiling, she realized once again he'd thrown her off balance. And offered her a chance at something extraordinary.

"Thanks, Josh. This'll be fun."

"It'll probably be tedious, boring and get old real fast. But if you're game, we leave at nine."

Michelle jumped up. "I better get to bed, then, so I can get up early and be ready to go. What should I wear?"

"Whatever you usually do if you're browsing around the Quarter. The key here is to make sure you don't look obvious."

He stacked the folders and held his hand for the one she'd been working on.

She brought it over almost dancing with excitement. This would be fun! And give her time with Josh.

He rose and switched off the lamp. When he turned, he almost bumped into Michelle.

She flung her arms around him and hugged him tightly.

"Thanks. This will be different, but exciting, don't you think?"

Josh resisted with every ounce of willpower he possessed. She hadn't a clue how difficult she made it for him to keep the distance he'd vowed to keep after last night. She wasn't interested, end of subject. Once he found her father, she'd be gone and wanted no complications to confuse the issue.

But it didn't feel like the end of the subject with her soft body pressed against his, with her arms holding him tightly. And her smile was enough to melt icebergs. How was one man to resist?

She almost had him considering extending the end of the relationship beyond what they'd agreed to, but he knew how that went. Hadn't he learned from Sylvia that he wasn't cut out for marriage? He had his daughter and once she was in school, they could establish a routine that'd see them through the years until she was grown and on her own.

Michelle stepped back, dropping her arms.

"Good night," she said and turned to hurry to the stairs.

Josh watched her go, feeling old and tired and lonely.

By five o'clock the next afternoon, Josh suspected Michelle was ready to throw in the towel.

They'd been pretending to be shopping at the one store

in the French Quarter all day. Fortunately, it was large and had an extensive inventory. Nevertheless, he knew he could itemize everything in the place from the lovely ceramic masks, to the elaborate be-feathered Mardi Gras masks to the tacky souvenirs lining the shelves right inside the door. He expected the day would cure Michelle of thinking the work of a private investigator was glamorous.

Josh showed none of the boredom he was feeling. He was annoyed the suspected family member hadn't shown up this day.

"Ready to leave?" he asked moving closer to Michelle.

"Yes."

He smiled at her enthusiastic response.

Josh called a good night to the owner and took Michelle's arm, leading her to the street.

"Want to get a bite to eat before we head for home?"

"Sure. Do you do this kind of thing a lot? It was a very long day."

She rotated one foot then the other to ease the ache.

"I used to when I was starting out. Now I have others who have less experience and can use the training. But every once in a while I like to do some field work myself. Keeps the edge, you know."

"Ummm. I wonder if the owner will ever find out who's passing the phony money," she said as they walked along Royal Street, heading toward Canal Street.

"I think so. It's just a matter of time. And careful surveillance."

As they reached busy Canal Street, one of the riverboats' whistles blew.

"Let's go see the boats," she said impulsively.

"We could see if there's room on the dinner cruise, have dinner aboard, if you like," Josh said as they sauntered in the late afternoon heat. "It'd be cooler on the river."

"I guess. It's exactly what Caroline suggested, dinner and dancing at some romantic restaurant. What could be more romantic than a riverboat dinner cruise?"

"Then you'll have something to tell her if she asks what we did today."

"It beats telling her I shopped all day and didn't buy a single thing."

The stern wheeler was crowded when they stepped aboard. Saturday nights combined locals with tourists. But the festive feeling was infectious. When the Dixieland music started, Michelle tapped out the rhythm with her toes.

"You like Dixieland?" Josh leaned closer to ask. He could smell the sweet fragrance of her hair. Another fact to learn about his wife.

She nodded, smiling brightly. "When I was a little girl, we'd hear the music from some of the boats as they moved up river. It sounded so bright and exciting. Grandmother never let Dixieland in her home. She preferred the classics."

"Then, I'm glad we came."

He enjoyed the look of pure bliss on her face. Another way to snub her grandmother. He was glad he never met the woman.

Being on the ship made it a lot easier to resist Michelle's allure with a couple of hundred other passengers around. He glanced at his watch. Another eighteen hours and Penny'd be home.

He could last until then. She made the perfect shield against anything personal developing between him and Michelle.

Dinner proved to be enjoyable. They shared a table with a couple from Texas and spent the meal exchanging stories about New Orleans and Dallas. When the last of the Bananas Foster had been consumed, Josh and Michelle went to the aft lounge to listen to the soft jazz that was now playing. Finding a couple of chairs near a dark corner, he put them together and sat beside her.

By the time the riverboat returned to the dock, Josh was ready to swim ashore. The cold river water would be perfect to quench the fire ignited by Michelle's presence. She did nothing that could be construed as provocative, unless he counted her breathing. But it didn't take much, he was coming to realize to turn him on. He enjoyed her company, liked finding out what made her laugh. She always seemed so naively startled to find she could do something she hadn't tried before. He knew he was growing cynical and it was refreshing to be with someone who was still wide-eyed and fascinated about the world.

It was late by the time they reached home. But Josh was too keyed up to sleep. He bid Michelle goodnight once they were inside and headed for the living room. There were still a few more records to get straight.

"Aren't you going to bed now?" she asked, pausing by the bottom step.

"I'll be up later."

"Thanks, Josh. This was a most interesting day."

He looked at her, struck by her tone. "But not one you want to repeat too often."

Hesitating a moment, she wrinkled her nose and slowly shook her head.

"I don't think so. My feet still ache and if I never see a souvenir of New Orleans again, it'll be too soon. I wish we could have caught the bad guy, though."

"We'll get him. Or the cops will. But it was a perfect day for showing you what a lot of my business is like. Next time, I'll wait until I have some surveillance going where we sit in the car all night."

"Please do. Thanks for taking me today. I liked the ending," she said as she turned to run lightly up the stairs.

He'd have liked the ending more if he were going up with her, he thought wryly. He leaned against the archway into the living room and just listened. He heard Michelle enter the bathroom and close the door behind her.

For a moment the memory of her in the bath flashed into mind. Guess there wouldn't be any more nights where she bathed by candlelight. At least not while he was home.

A few minutes later he heard her cross the hall to her room and again close the door.

Shaking his head, he pushed off from the wall and headed for the small stack of folders that waited. If he couldn't sleep, he might as well be productive!

Michelle knew she'd blown it. Sunday morning and here she sat sipping coffee alone. Idly she twisted around the muffin she nibbled on. She wasn't hungry. Sipping the coffee was about the limit of her interest in sustenance.

Josh walked in and when she looked up, she caught her breath. He'd obviously just finished his shower. His hair was still damp, and his face freshly shaved. The echo of the words he'd once said to her applied here. *He looked good enough to eat!*

He pulled out a chair, turned it around and straddled it, resting his arms on the high back.

"Penny will be home soon," he said.

She nodded.

"I expect Caroline and Brandon will bring her in."

"I guess so."

"Which means we'll have to play our charade again. Just wanted to make sure that's what you wanted."

Licking her lip, Michelle nodded. "If you don't mind."

Josh shook his head, his eyes boring into hers. "Once your sister's gone, I thought I'd take Penny swimming. We'll be out of your hair this afternoon."

Michelle's heart sank. He didn't even want to be around her. Maybe she should throw caution to the wind and agree to his suggestion. It couldn't hurt any more than if she didn't. She was fast falling in love with the man.

Maybe she should grab for whatever happiness she could find and let the future take care of itself.

Only, now, she didn't have a clue how to bring it up. He hadn't mentioned it again. Had he changed his mind?

"You two don't have to leave on my account."

He shrugged. "It's no hardship. Penny likes to swim. Want us to get dinner out?"

"No, I've already planned dinner."

She wished he'd invite her to go swimming with them. But apparently the conversation was over. He rose, replaced the chair and left.

Feeling inadequate and dejected, Michelle went to dress for the day. Maybe between now and the time they left, Josh would invite her to join them.

He didn't.

Brandon brought Penny home, explaining that Caroline was feeling tired and he'd insisted she stay in bed.

"I thought watching Penny would be too much," Michelle said, worried for her sister.

"No, it wasn't. We had a great time. But Caroline and I were up late last night and I just thought she should rest today. We'd like to have Penny come stay with us again sometime soon."

"Maybe after your own baby is born," Josh said.

They all were at the front door, Brandon having declined to enter.

"We'll want to have her visit again long before that," Brandon said, before turning to head for his car.

"Have fun, kid?" Josh asked.

Penny exuberantly explained her visit. Before Michelle could hear all she had to say, Josh suggested swimming, which immediately changed the direction of Penny's thoughts. She ran upstairs to find her bathing suit and in only moments, she and her father left.

Michelle watched them drive away.

He hadn't asked her.

And she hadn't invited herself along.

Now what was she going to do for the rest of the day? Dinner wouldn't take long to prepare. She could do laundry and vacuum the house, but the feeling of belonging she'd experienced last week was missing.

She wanted to be with Josh, pure and simple.

By the following Wednesday Michelle was about at the end of her rope. Any thought of keeping her distance from Josh had long since faded. And yet she was unable to draw closer. It was as if he'd erected an invisible wall between them. Nothing she said seemed to breach it.

Maybe plain speaking was called for. Tonight she'd wait until Penny was in bed, and then tell Josh she'd changed her mind. She didn't want to continue as they had over the last two days. If he still wanted her, then—

When her desk phone rang, Michelle almost snatched it up. She kept hoping the next call would be Josh.

It wasn't. It was Mrs. Robinson at the day care.

"Mrs. O'Malley, we need you down here. There's been an accident."

Chapter Nine

"An accident? What happened?" Fear clutched her. "I'm afraid Penny fell and cut herself quite badly. We've called for an ambulance but she's crying for her father. Can you notify him and then come down?"

"I'll be there in two minutes."

Quickly, Michelle hung up, then picked up her phone and dialed Josh's work number from memory as she grabbed her purse and headed down to the day care.

The temp answered. What was her name? Michelle couldn't remember.

"I need to speak with Josh, please. It's an emergency," she said, as she dashed for the elevator.

"He's not available right now. What happened? Can I take a message? I'll try to locate him."

"Tell him his wife called. There's been an accident and Penny's been hurt. I'm going with her to the hospital. I'll call him from there."

When she entered the day care facility a couple of minutes later she spotted Penny immediately. One of the teachers held her, pressing a white cloth to her head. The little girl was crying, calling for her daddy. Blood splattered over her play suit and along the side of her head.

Michelle almost burst into tears at the sight.

"Oh, Penny, honey, what happened?" She reached for her and Penny lunged into her arms.

"Michelle, I gots hurt."

"I can see that, honey. What happened?" She raised her gaze to the teacher.

"She was playing on the slide and took a tumble over the side. We found some rocks on the playground that shouldn't have been there. I think one of them caused the gash. She'll be fine, but we called an ambulance. She needs to be checked out by a doctor to make sure."

"Shh, honey, I know it hurts, but you're going to be all right," Michelle crooned as she hugged Penny tightly and rocked her back and forth. The little girl continued to cry, but she stopped calling for her father and snuggled against Michelle.

"I'm glad you comed, Michelle. I was a-scared."

"Of course I came, darling. As soon as they called me. I'm so sorry you're hurt. Your daddy will be here as soon as he can make it."

In a whirlwind of activity they were transported to Liberty Hospital. The young doctor in the emergency room soon had Penny cleaned up and placed two small stitches in the gash near her hairline.

Giving her a tetanus shot, he pronounced her fit as a fiddle.

"Or she will be in a couple of days. I expect she'll be achy and show some bruises. But this kind of thing happens all the time with kids. Don't worry, Mrs. O'Malley, she'll be fine. How are you doing?"

Michelle tried to respond intelligently, but she felt shaky.

"Michelle?" a familiar voice roared.

"In here, Josh," she called, moving to peer through the opening in the curtain. "We're in here."

She was so glad to see him when he walked in.

"Daddy!" Penny called, struggling to sit up on the high examination table.

"Easy, kiddo." The doctor assisted her to sit and Josh swept her into his arms.

"Is she okay?" he asked the doctor.

"She'll be fine. I was telling your wife, she'll be achy for a few days and probably sport some colorful bruises, but there is no concussion, no broken bones."

Josh turned and saw Michelle. Without a word, he crossed to her and put his free arm around her shoulders, pulling her tightly against him.

"I'm sorry, Josh. She fell on the playground."

"This kind of thing happens with kids, honey. Not your fault. How are you doing? You're as pale as a ghost."

"I'm fine. Do you suppose they weren't watching her closely enough at the day care?"

"No, what I think is this is just one of a long line of accidents we're likely to face as she grows up. I had my share of visits to the emergency room and doctor's office as a kid, didn't you?"

Michelle shook her head.

Josh tightened his grip. "Well, if your grandmother hadn't constrained you so much you would have! Are we ready to go?" He looked at the doctor.

The man wrote a prescription, ripped the sheet off the pad and held it out. "Get this filled and give a tablet to Penny if she complains about headaches. Otherwise, keep her quiet for a day or two. She'll be fine. Have her regular doctor see her in a week. The stitches will be ready to come out by then."

"Thanks."

Michelle reluctantly turned from the comfort of Josh's embrace and tried to smile at the young doctor. But her heart sank as she followed Josh. Adrenaline let-down, she tried to tell herself as they left the hospital.

They headed for Josh's car. He spoke softly to Penny as she rested her head against his shoulder.

Michelle felt totally helpless. And guilty. Maybe the child care situation at her work wasn't safe. Had she put Penny in danger by offering that solution to Josh?

Once settled in the car, Josh glanced at her as he started the engine. "You okay?"

She nodded. "I was so scared."

"Yeah, so was I the first couple of times."

Michelle swung her head around to stare at him in startled surprise. *"The first couple of times?"*

He pulled out of the parking lot and merged with the flow of traffic.

"Adventuresome kids get into trouble. Fact of life. But when she first came to live with me, I didn't know it. She skinned her knees when she was trying to race one of the kids in the neighborhood. I wanted to forbid her to ever set foot out of her room—at least until she was thirty or something. To keep her safe, you know?"

Michelle nodded.

"But that's unrealistic. Joanne at work, who's the mother of three boys, set me straight. When Penny's finger was smashed by a neighbor's child dropping a rock on it, I was able to handle it much better. But I have to tell you, you never get completely complacent about it."

"She's so little. Maybe she shouldn't go on slides yet. Do you think the day care is a mistake? Maybe I should stay home and watch her."

He flicked her a quick look.

"No, you don't. She's fine at day care. She loves playing with the other children. Think how much she talks about them at dinner every night. She'll be fine, Michelle."

Checking on Penny, Michelle blinked away tears. The little girl looked so small in the car seat. The bandage was a stark white on her head. Dirt and blood stained her clothes. She was fast asleep.

"Hey," Josh reached out to take Michelle's hand. "She'll be fine. Welcome to the world of parenting."

"I think you should reconsider your idea of keeping her in her room until she's thirty. Sounds pretty good to me."

He chuckled and squeezed gently. "You'll toughen up."

Michelle doubted it. Even if she had time. But in all likelihood she'd be gone from their lives before the next mishap occurred.

Despite being scared to death when she ran into that day care center this afternoon, Michelle knew she'd miss being a part of Penny's life—no matter what happened.

The warmth from Josh's hand began to seep into her.

He had the ability to make her forget everything. She wondered how far along he'd gotten in his search for her father. If it took forever, that'd probably suit her.

What if he never found him?

Instead of the old familiar frustration at not knowing more about her father, Michelle began to imagine he was lost forever. And she'd stay with Josh until they were both old and gray. Every few months he'd come home and tell her that he still had no clues. She'd have to pretend to care. But the truth was, the quest had taken a backseat to what was important to her now.

She still felt shaky. Maybe her emotions were too suspect. She couldn't be falling in love with Josh.

When they reached the house, Josh scooped Penny up and carried her inside.

"I'll give her a bath and put her down for a nap," he said as Michelle unlocked the front door.

"I can help."

"No need. You'll want to get cleaned up yourself. I can manage." He strode up the stairs, carrying his daughter as if she weighed nothing.

Michelle watched them, once again feeling left out. Was she always going to be on the outside looking in?

She went to her room to don a cool dress and slip into sandals. She felt exhausted. Hearing their laughter reassured her as nothing else had. Penny *would* be all right.

But would she?

Michelle peeked into the door to Penny's room, watching silently as Josh rocked Penny in his arms. He was so big and the little girl looked particularly small when cradled in her daddy's arms. Love blossomed in Michelle's heart as she studied the two of them. There was something special about a strong man holding a child so tenderly.

"Is she all right?" she asked when Josh noticed her in the doorway.

"Almost asleep," he said.

Penny smiled sleepily at Michelle.

It was at that moment Michelle realized she couldn't love Penny any more if she were her own child. Raising her gaze to Josh, she knew without a doubt she loved them both.

"I'll start dinner," she said and turned to flee.

If only she could outrun her emotions.

"Dumb move, Michelle," she said a few minutes later as she drew the meat from the refrigerator. "Josh's made it clear more than once that he's not in this for the long haul."

"What are you muttering about?" Josh asked as he walked into the kitchen.

He hadn't heard, had he? Michelle eyed him warily. "Nothing, just mumbling. She asleep?"

"Yes. And as late as it is, she might sleep through the night."

"She didn't get any dinner."

"She'll ask for something if she wakes up. I think sleep's better for her right now."

Josh pulled out a chair and sat down with a tired sigh. Stretching out his long legs, he tilted back on the rear legs of the chair and slipped his hands in his pockets. "Penny was glad you showed up when I didn't."

"She kept calling for you, they said, but she stopped when I got there. Not quite the same as her daddy, but an adequate substitute, I guess."

"No doubt about it. Thanks. I owe you."

Michelle shook her head. "Just my job, right?"

Josh was silent for a long time. "Yeah, I guess."

She looked over at his tone, but he appeared lost in thought. Worried about his daughter, she suspected.

Dinner was quiet without Penny's chatter. Once finished, Josh offered to help with the dishes.

"Not necessary. There are only a few, I'll be done in no time," Michelle said, rising to clear the table.

At loose ends, Josh wandered outside. Turning on the sprinklers, he watched as the water caught the waning light of the setting sun, showering rainbows everywhere. Feeling restless and unsettled, he didn't want to watch television. Might as well watch the water spray.

He hadn't brought any more work home. They were caught up, thanks to Michelle's assistance.

Only part of the job, she'd say.

Which was how she viewed being married to him. Leaning against the post on the porch, he watched a car slowly drive by. She'd rebuffed all attempts to change the status of their marriage. How clear could a woman make it that she wasn't interested?

But it didn't stop the desire that rose whenever she was around. And it wasn't just that. He loved hearing her laughter, seeing the startled awareness in her eyes when she discovered something new. Seeing the innocent delight she took in being with Penny.

She was good with Penny, too. Listened to her and didn't treat her like an inconvenience.

He hadn't planned on getting married again after failing before. But now that they were married, it wasn't proving as difficult as he'd expected.

Of course not, it wasn't a real marriage. Michelle looked on it as a job. A temporary situation until he found her father and Caroline had her baby. Then she'd take off.

Josh wasn't sure what he wanted, but it looked more and more as if he didn't want Michelle to leave.

"No work tonight?" Michelle asked as she pushed open the screen door and joined him on the porch.

"No. With the next billing cycle, I think we'll be all caught up. Thanks for your help."

"I enjoyed it. If you need some extra assistance anytime, let me know."

She came to stand near him. Too near. He could smell the sweet scent she wore. Light and fragrant, he'd forever associate it with Michelle.

"It's so hot tonight," she said, sitting on the top step.

Josh sat beside her, forgetting every resolution to keep his distance. He'd take what he could get.

"The house's cool," he said, still watching the water spray. The sun had set. Twilight cloaked the neighborhood. Lights in the windows of the neighbors' houses shone a warm yellow in the night.

"I know, but I like sitting out. We didn't use the air conditioner a lot when I was younger. So my sisters and I used to walk along the river for whatever breeze was blowing. The spray from the sprinklers would feel good," she said wistfully.

"So go play in it."

Michelle looked at him with those wide eyes of hers. Josh felt like he'd been hit with a truck. How long did she think he could resist?

"I'd get soaked. The spray is too high to just go wading."

"So, that dress is washable. It'd cool you off."

Josh could almost see her thought process as she eyed the sprinklers. The temptation was great, he could tell. He wished she felt as tempted by him.

"That would look great to the neighbors, right? Me cavorting like a four-year-old in the sprinklers," she said slowly.

He smiled. "They can't see anything. It's dark, and the tree casts shadows from the moonlight. Not that I think the neighbors would be outside now anyway. They're all tucked up in their cool homes, windows closed, TV on."

Josh watched as Michelle scooted off her sandals. She rose and glanced at him.

"Don't you want to cool off?"

He hadn't expected her to invite him. "Sure, I'll take off my shoes. You go on."

He kicked off the running shoes and stood, pulling the shirt off his back. The sultry heat of New Orleans in the summer often had him wishing he could wear less. Tossing the shirt on the steps beside their shoes, he watched as she dallied at the outer fringes of the spray. She almost danced in the water.

Josh took a deep breath and let out a rebel yell, running into the spray, he swooped Michelle up and swung her around and around in the cascading water.

The shock of cold water made her gasp and she let out a yell.

"Josh! Have you lost your mind? This water is freezing! Put me down!" But her giggles belied the words "When you're cooled off. It's great!"

He set her on her feet, but kept an arm around her shoulder. The fine spray of the sprinklers soaked them both. Michelle's dress molded her figure. Now he wished he'd put on the porch light.

"I'm cool," she laughed, holding her hand out to try to keep the spray from soaking her face. Her hair dripped, hung in wet strands. Suddenly she raised her hands above her head and danced again on the grass, the spray covering them both.

Desire hit suddenly and hard. Josh caught the laughter as he reached out and pulled her closer, his mouth covering hers. He kissed her, savoring every speck of reaction she gave, pulling her cooled body against his bare chest, ignoring the water that cascaded over them. It no longer felt cool, now it was cold against his heated skin.

When he raised his head, Michelle didn't move. But he could see her wide eyes gazing up into his.

"I want you, Michelle," he said.

What an ineffective statement. He yearned for her, craved her. Needed to know everything about her, from where she liked to be touched to how she slept at night. Her taste inflamed him, her scent nearly drove him to his knees.

He'd never experienced this with another woman. Why Michelle?

And what was she going to do now?

"Michelle?" His lips touched hers again, trailed slow kisses across her cheek and nibbled gently against her earlobe. Her hands twisted themselves behind his neck and she pressed against him.

Her fingers began tracing patterns against his hot skin. She let one hand skim across his bare shoulder and down his muscular chest. She was driving him crazy.

"Say yes, Michelle." He kissed her again and prayed she'd say yes.

"Yes, Josh," she whispered.

He heard her. Sweeping her up into his arms, he headed for the porch.

"I'd love to make love to you beneath the stars, but I want our first time to be special, not complicated by leaves and twigs," he said, mounting the shallow steps that led to the porch.

The cold air in the house sent an instant chill through them both and she snuggled closer. "Guess that sprinkler cooled me down," she murmured, daring to kiss his jaw, let her lips move across his shoulder.

Josh carried her into his room and nudged the door shut with his shoulder. Standing her beside the bed, he kissed her again. Grateful her hands were still locked around his neck, he knew she was fully involved.

"You need to get out of those wet clothes," he said softly, already beginning to unfasten the buttons that kept the dress closed.

"I guess you seem to have a head start on me," she said, lightly running her fingertips over the muscles of his chest.

"Oh, honey, if you want to drive me insane, do that one more time," he said, batting her hands away and peeling the dress from her shoulders.

She sought to get closer to Josh.

"Let me shuck these jeans," he said. The rasp of the zipper sounded. Then he heard another sound.

"What's that?" Michelle asked, looking around.

"The baby monitor. I use it to keep track of Penny during the night. If she wakes up and calls, I can hear her in here."

"Is it a two-way setup?" she asked.

"No, she can't hear us. Anyway, she's sound asleep."

Before she could say anything more, he kissed her again.

Michelle woke slowly, moving restlessly. Opening her eyes, she stared at the pillow next to hers. An indentation showed where Josh had slept, but he had already gone.

Slowly she sat up, feeling awkward. . Rising, she picked up her dress which was still damp. Wrinkling her nose, she held it in one hand. No way was she going to put it on. She pulled the sheet from the bed and wrapped it around her for the short trip to her own bedroom.

The house was silent. On the way to her room, she peeked into Penny's. The little girl lay on her stomach, still fast asleep.

Maybe it wasn't as late as she thought it was, Michelle mused as she hurried into her room. The clock said seven fifteen. Why had Josh gotten up so early? Was he downstairs? Or did he have an early appointment? She had time before she needed to get to work, or should she stay home with Penny today?

Gathering her things, she headed for the bathroom. The warm shower felt good. Dressed a short time later, she again checked on Penny, then went to the kitchen. She'd make pancakes for the little girl and see how she felt about going to the day care today. If she wasn't up to it, Michelle would skip work, as well.

But Penny seemed raring to go a few minutes later when she whirled into the kitchen.

"Hi, Michelle. Did you see my stitches. I gots two!"

"Have, honey. You *have* two. And yes, I saw the doctor put them in." And hoped never to go through something like that again. Michelle truly thought it hurt her more than Penny. The child had a local anesthetic, after all.

"Where's Daddy?"

"Gone to work, I guess."

She found the note leaning against the milk carton when she opened the refrigerator. Her heart skipped a beat and Michelle reached for it. He hadn't left without a word, just put the note where she was sure not to miss it.

Lunch around noon?

"Short and to the point," she murmured. What had she expected, protestations of undying love? Just because—

"I'm hungry," Penny said.

Michelle slipped the note into her pocket and began to fix breakfast. But she couldn't slip away from the tingling sensation of anticipation that curled within. The warm glow that seemed to fill her. Josh wanted to see her again at lunch! He didn't even want to wait until after work. That had to mean something, right?

She called once she reached work to let him know she'd be there. And update him on how Penny was doing. As far as she could tell, the little girl was totally fine and not traumatized in the least by yesterday's accident.

It was ten minutes after twelve when Michelle entered the investigative offices. She remembered the first time she'd come, how he'd been so impatient to leave to get Penny. So much had changed since then. Yet it had only been a few weeks.

"Hi, Mrs. O'Malley," the receptionist said with a warm welcome on her face.

"Hi." Darn, she couldn't remember the woman's name. "I've come to have lunch with Josh. Is he here?"

"He'll be back soon. He had to go out on a case a couple of hours ago. I know he remembered lunch with you. Would you like to wait in his office?"

"Okay." Michelle followed the young woman into Josh's private office, and gazed around. She'd been in it a couple of times, but just for fleeting visits. Glancing at the different stacks of folders on the desk and credenza, she wondered if he were truly all caught up on the accounts.

Idly moving around, she glanced at two of the stacks. A name caught her eye from a label on a folder midway down the smaller pile. *Sam Williams.*

"Are these accounts awaiting billing?" she asked, looking closer.

"Naw, those are the inactive accounts," the receptionist replied.

"Inactive?" Michelle repeated, puzzled. Wasn't that folder for her father?

"Yes, cases that we're no longer working on for one reason or another."

Chapter Ten

Michelle couldn't move. She glanced at the receptionist, but the woman was already walking back to her desk. When she was out of sight, Michelle shifted the top folders and picked up the one labeled Sam Williams. She went around the desk and sat in his chair, opening the folder. There were notes and photocopies of faxes. Scanning the loose paper quickly, she flipped to the report sheet stapled to the back of the folder. She knew how he set up the folders, hadn't she worked on enough of them?

From the reports, it looked as if Josh had located several men who matched some or all of the sketchy information they had. But he'd said nothing to her about progress. And the final note on the file was over a week old.

What was the folder doing in the inactive stack? A mistake?

A cold feeling settled on Michelle.

Or had Josh deliberately decided to hold off in locating her father to make sure she stuck around to take care of Penny?

Once the thought popped into her mind, she couldn't shake it.

Last night—had that also been about keeping her around? Watching a four-year-old was difficult when a man had to earn a living and had no one to back him up when work overlapped into Penny's child care limits. She understood a man being desperate to keep whatever child care he could.

Feeling sick, Michelle took a deep breath unable to believe he'd stopped work on the search. There had to be some sort of explanation. She believed she could trust him. She depended upon him to do his best to locate her father.

Now she questioned that. She had lied to her sisters and friends and work, pretending to be married, pretending to be in love—all because she trusted him.

Only, it hadn't all been pretense. Not for her.

Michelle didn't know how long she sat there, her mind spinning with different scenarios. None satisfied her. She had the proof in black and white in front of her.

"Hi Michelle, sorry I'm late. I thought I'd be finished before—"

Josh breezed into the office. When he caught sight of her, he stopped abruptly.

Michelle looked up. His face said it all. He dropped his gaze to the opened folder, glanced at the stack of inactive files, then raised his gaze to hers, guilt evident.

Slowly he closed the door behind him, shutting the two of them in his office.

"I can explain," he said.

"I can't wait to hear. This is the folder for my father, right?" she asked, closing it and resting her hands on it.

"Yes."

"I found it in the inactive pile."

"Temporarily," he said, stepping closer. He never took his gaze from her.

"So the search was suspended."

"Temporarily," he said again.

"Why?"

Josh rubbed the back of his neck, glancing around the cluttered office as if searching for inspiration.

Michelle stood, feeling at a disadvantage sitting. Her heart pounded as she waited for Josh to explain away what she suspected. To have him tell her the folder was in the wrong pile.

So far he hadn't.

"It isn't going to take much longer to narrow the field to the right man," he began. "I guess you read the file?"

She nodded.

"A quick trip to each location, ask a few pointed questions, and we'll be able to verify his identity in no time."

"Then why hasn't it been done already?" she asked, keeping her voice even. She refused to let him know how much the discovery hurt her. She felt betrayed. After all she'd done, she deserved more than this.

"Why did you stop the investigation over a week ago?"

He met her eyes again. "Initially because I needed you to stay with Penny."

"That was our bargain. I fulfilled my part." Tears threatened. She'd done everything just as they had agreed. Why hadn't he?

"Was keeping a temporary mother so important you'd deliberately delay the search to make sure I didn't leave? I said I'd stay until Caroline had her baby and Penny was settled at school."

He nodded, drew in a deep breath. "You said that, but I wasn't sure once you had what you wanted you'd stay. I only need a few more months. You haven't known about your father all these years, would a few more months hurt?"

"Rather than give me the chance to decide that, you made sure things went exactly as you wanted by halting the investigation. I thought better of you, Josh." She picked up the folder and skirted the desk, heading for the door.

"Wait, Michelle, there's more."

"After last night, I guess there's more. How low can a man get?"

She pushed past him and almost ran from the office. She didn't hesitate a second when Josh called after her.

The elevator was on the floor, its doors about to shut. Squeezing in at the last second, Michelle pushed the down button. She could hear Josh's voice through the doors just before the car began its descent.

When she reached the sidewalk, she started walking. Her thoughts tumbled. She couldn't focus on anything and yet she needed to think. Try to understand what was going on. And decide what she would do about it. Obviously last night hadn't been the glorious revelation to Josh that she'd experienced. In light of what she learned today, it had to have been a ploy to keep her tied to him.

At least until he had Penny situated.

It was stupid to think otherwise. He'd always been honest—he wanted her for an affair. He'd never said anything about love.

Tears threatened again.

"You didn't have to go that far," she said aloud. Two people looked at her oddly as they passed.

She'd believed something special was building between her and Josh, certain that the strong feelings she experienced couldn't have been totally one-sided.

Yet she'd obviously seen only what she wanted to see.

He didn't even care enough for her or their deal to complete the search for her father.

Anger burned at his callous disregard toward their deal. She'd never have left him in the lurch. She wasn't Sylvia. She wasn't anyone except herself, Michelle Talmadge O'Malley.

The afternoon sun beat relentlessly on her as she walked. When she realized how hot she was, she took stock. Instinct, she thought, when she recognized where she was. Only a few blocks from Abby's place. Quickly she headed for her sister's apartment, trying to remember if this was one of her days off. She needed family now. The time for pretending she'd found happiness with Josh was over.

She didn't know what they'd tell Caroline, but for now, she needed someone to talk to, to confide in. Someone who wouldn't betray her for his own selfish interests. Who wouldn't lead her on and then let her discover it was all for his own purpose with no consideration for her own feelings.

How could she have fallen in love with a man who used

people? How could she still wish he could explain. If he'd just said it was misplaced, she'd probably believed him.

Abby opened the door when Michelle rang the bell. Thank goodness for rotating shifts.

"Hi Michelle, you just caught me." Taking a closer look, she reached out to gently grasp Michelle's arm and draw her into the cool apartment. "You look awful. What's wrong?"

At her kind tone, Michelle burst into tears.

"Gee, I guess this isn't a friendly little visit in the middle of a work day," Abby said hugging her sister. "Come and sit down. Tell Abby all about it."

Grabbing a handful of tissues in passing, Abby led her to the sofa and urged her to sit. Stuffing the tissues into one hand, she took the folder and dropped it onto the coffee table.

"Sorry, I don't usually lose control like this," Michelle said as she tried to dry her eyes. "It must be the heat."

"Uh-huh," Abby agreed.

"Or the humidity."

"Uh-huh."

"It's Josh," Michelle said, giving up all thought of further pretense.

"Figures."

"What?" She looked up, drying the last of the tears. He was not worth crying over!

"Well, you're usually composed and handle things fine. To be in such a state, I figured it had to be your husband. What happened, you two have a fight?"

"No. But I found out he's not the man I thought he was."

"Who is he, then?" Abby asked, surprised.

"He's a lying, deceitful, selfish, self-serving man. He does nice things, but not to be nice, just to lure me in, make me feel comfortable. To give me hope. Then he stops for no reason except he thinks I'm like his first wife. Which I'm not, but would he let me prove it, oh, no, he made all the decisions and hid everything from me until I found out. Then he didn't lie, just kept looking at me like he wanted to make something up, but of course he can't by now, could he?"

Abby blinked, and sat down on a chair. "I'm not following this, Michelle," she said slowly.

"The proof is in the folder. The one from the *inactive* pile." Michelle picked up the folder and tossed it to her sister. "I can't believe I let myself believe him. Pretended it might all come right one day. That a man like that could really fall for a woman like me."

"Huh? Now what are you talking about?" Abby asked as she skimmed through the various sheets in the folder. "Has Josh located our father?" she asked excitedly.

Michelle surged to her feet and began to pace. "Is that all you can say? My heart's broken and you ask if he's located our father?"

Abby's head snapped up at that and she stared at Michelle. "Why is your heart broken?"

"I just explained!"

"No, you didn't. Sit down and tell me, and go slow. I haven't understood a word you've said since you arrived."

Michelle tossed the spent tissues into a wastebasket and

calmly sat on the sofa. Explaining to Abby proved harder than she'd expected. But she covered the entire situation, from the earlier attempts to hire a private investigator until she found the folder. Except for last night. That was too personal.

"Wow, Michelle. I'd never have expected it of you. Good going!"

"What?"

"That was brilliant, getting him to search for our father. And the cover up was super. I never suspected, and I know Caroline didn't doesn't whatever. So what's the problem?"

"He stopped looking for our father."

"Temporarily, he said. Just tell him you'll stay until Penny's set and he'll resume where he left off."

"He should have known I'd stay. I said I would." Especially after last night, she'd stay.

Abby looked at her a moment. "Uh-oh, I just had a thought. Penny won't stay your stepdaughter when you two separate. Darn, I really like that little girl."

"Me, too," Michelle said, wondering if the tears would overtake her again.

"I think Josh likes you," Abby said gently.

Michelle shrugged, suddenly listless. She leaned back against the sofa cushions. She couldn't believe she'd gone from feeling on top of the world this morning to feeling used and discarded this afternoon.

The phone rang.

Abby picked it up and spoke briefly. Michelle didn't pay attention. She was trying to figure out what to do next.

Maybe she could room with Abby until the sublet was up on her apartment. She'd have to come up with some story for Caroline, but she could figure that out later.

"Okay, I'll see you in a few minutes."

Michelle looked at her as Abby hung up.

"Who was that?"

"Josh. He's coming here to see you."

"No!" She jumped up. "I don't want to see him! I'm getting out of here."

"Wait a minute, Michelle. Give the guy a break. Hear him out. You owe him that much."

"I don't."

"What can it hurt?"

Michelle sighed. She couldn't hurt any more than she already did.

And she did have to talk to him to arrange to get her things from his home.

What about Penny? She couldn't just leave without saying goodbye. In fact, Michelle thought, maybe she shouldn't leave at all. At least not until school started. That'd show Josh that his distrust had been misplaced. That she could be counted on to uphold her end of the bargain no matter what!

"Go wash your face, I'll let him in if he gets here before you're finished," Abby said.

Feeling refreshed and ready to face the world some time later, Michelle walked into the living room, and stopped when she saw Josh.

"Abby went for a walk," he said, rising when she entered.

"It's hot out."

"She won't melt. I couldn't catch the elevator."

"How did you know I'd be here?"

He gave a half smile. "I'm a great P.I., remember? Isn't that why you came to me in the first place?"

Michelle could scarcely remember why she'd gone to Josh's office that first day. She only wished now that she hadn't.

No, that wasn't strictly true. She just wished she hadn't fallen in love with him.

"Sit down, Josh. Your towering over me makes me nervous."

"Good, then maybe I won't be the only one nervous here."

Startled, Michelle's gaze clashed with his. "You've never been nervous a day in your life."

He'd been so calm when dealing with Penny and her injury, with playing the role of devoted bridegroom, when handling Brandon's inquisition.

"Try scared silly," he said stepping closer.

"About what?"

"That I blew things beyond repair."

She shrugged, watching him warily.

Slowly, as if not to frighten a scared puppy, he reached out his hand and cupped the back of her head.

Michelle stiffened. "Don't."

"Michelle, last night was special. But it wasn't the only special part of our relationship. Just being with you is special."

She closed her eyes. Maybe if she didn't have to look at him, she could think straight.

"You don't need to sweet-talk me any more, Josh. I've said I'll stay until after Caroline has her baby, and by then Penny will be settled into her after-school care."

"Good. Then there's just us to discuss."

"There is no us." She opened her eyes and glared up into his. "I can't believe you stopped the investigation."

"I wanted you to stay," he said simply. "I was afraid that if I fulfilled my end of the bargain, you'd take off. Would it hurt to stall a little longer? You said you just wanted to know about your dad, where he was, what he was doing. A few months one way or another wouldn't matter, would they? Not after all this time."

"I trusted you. I depended on you to uphold your end of the bargain."

"And I will. We didn't discuss time frames. If I deliver the goods by November, I'll have done my part, right?"

His other arm came around her shoulders, drawing her closer and closer until Michelle put her palms up against his chest to keep some space between them. Only the minute she touched the warmth of his shirt, she longed to cling, not push.

Which reminded her of last night.

Which instigated the pain she'd felt earlier.

"You didn't have to resort to making love to keep me around," she muttered, her gaze dropping to the column of his throat. The pulse point beat in time to his heart. She had

the oddest notion to kiss him and feel that pulse against her
lips.

Josh made a sound that was half laugh, half groan.
"Resort to? Michelle, I've wanted you for weeks. Last night
was just a man at the end of his tether. It had nothing to do
with anything else but how we feel about each other and you
know it."

"I don't know anything of the sort. How do you feel
about me?" she asked, her own heart starting to pound.

"How do you feel about me?" he countered. Slowly she
let her gaze meet his. Almost holding her breath she
wondered if—

"You're the hot-shot P.I., you tell me."

"Babe, you've got me so mixed up I'm lucky I can put
my shoes on in the mornings. I can't begin to guess how you
feel about me, because I'm so caught up with feelings and
emotions that I never expected to experience. I love you,
Michelle O'Malley. I fought against it, denied it as long as I
could. Then I didn't want to frighten you off. That hadn't
been part of our agreement, but it didn't matter. I wanted
you last night. I still want you. So now you know."

Michelle stared at him in shock for several minutes.
Then she slipped her hands up and around his neck. "You
really love me? The man who never planned to marry again?
The man who swore off women for good, except as a baby-
sitter for his daughter?"

Resting his forehead against hers, he nodded.

"I can tell you're going to be the kind of wife who says I
told you so."

She laughed, her heart soaring. "Josh, I love you too!"
He almost crushed her in his embrace, his mouth finding
hers in a searing kiss.

"Truly?" he asked a few minutes later, searching her eyes
for the sincerity she knew he'd find.

"Yes, truly. But I didn't want you to know. I remember
all the times you said you didn't want to marry."

"Before I met you, honey. Before I knew you. Stay
married to me, Michelle. Let's make a lifetime together."

"Oh, Josh, yes!" Michelle tightened her grip and kissed
him, trying to show him with a single kiss all the love she had
for the man of her dreams. He wouldn't always be easy to
live with, but she wouldn't have any other.

She pulled back and smiled brightly. "Let's go get Penny
and tell her."

He nodded, releasing her slowly. "Not that she'll get the
distinction. She didn't know this was a temporary
arrangement."

"No, but I'd like to see her, just the same." She looked at
him uncertainly, wistfully. "Do you think maybe down the
road we could have her call me Mommy?"

"I expect she'll be delighted to start before the next baby
comes."

"Next baby?"

"You didn't want Caroline to be the only one having a
baby, did you? Penny can be the big cousin, but wouldn't
you like another, one of your very own?"

"Penny will be my very own, the child of my heart. I

love her, Josh. But yes, I wouldn't mind a whole houseful of kids. And in my house they'll get to run and yell and get dirty and have a dog and everything."

"Slide down banisters and learn manners at an early age."

"That, too," she said, reaching out to touch the future. Her future was Josh.

Epilogue

"I want to see, I want to see," Penny yelled, jumping up and down.

"You'll get to see, let Michelle open it first," Josh said as he handed Michelle the fancy wrapped box.

"What it is?" Michelle asked, reaching up to give her husband a quick kiss. She and Penny had been home just a few minutes when he walked in.

"Just a little *lagniappe*. See if you like it."

Michelle smiled and walked into the living room. The anticipation built as she delayed. Sitting on the sofa, she gave Josh a quick glance. A little gift. Her first from Josh, how could she not love it.

She slipped her finger beneath the edge of the wrapping paper.

In only a moment she withdrew the framed photograph. It was of the two of them on their wedding day. Tears of delight threatened as she traced the line of Josh's jaw. They looked radiant, just like any couple marrying should look on their special day.

"Wherever did you get this?"

"Your friend Bethany took a whole slough of pictures,

don't you remember. She asked me if I wanted to have some large copies. I liked that one best."

"And you have the others?"

"All of them. I didn't know if you'd want to see them. But they are her gift to us, and a surprise for you. Do you like it?"

"I love it!"

"If you like, I thought we could put it up somewhere," he said diffidently.

"I love it. Almost as much as I love you," she said softly as he sat beside her. Penny crowded on the other side.

"I want to see, Mommy. I want to see," Penny said, pulling on Michelle's arm.

Still not used to being called Mommy, Michelle felt a warmth in her heart. The same warmth she felt every time she met her husband's eyes.

Michelle showed her daughter the picture, remembering that day. How things had changed. She was loved and loved. She was no longer on the outside looking in.

"Oh, Josh, Abby called earlier. She still has the folder on our father and said to tell you she'll bring it in to the office tomorrow. I meant to tell you before, but I forgot."

Two small palms bracketed Michelle's cheeks as Penny stood beside her and turned her face. "For*have*, Mommy, don't say got."

Josh burst out laughing at Michelle's stunned expression.

"Explain that one away," Josh dared.

Instead, she gathered the little girl in her arms and

turned to Josh, all the love in her shining from her eyes. "I'll just count my blessings instead."

At those words, he leaned over to kiss her and Michelle knew she didn't need to find her father to complete her life. It was complete with Josh.

—The End—

Did you enjoy this story?
If so you may enjoy the next book in *The Talmadge Sisters*
series, **Trusting Abby** or you might like **Because of You**

More books by Barbara McMahon

The Talmadge Sisters
Letters to Caroline
Michelle's Marriage Deal
Trusting Abby

The Harts of Texas Series
Rebel Heart
Tangled Hearts
Reckless Heart

Cowboy Heroes Series
Blue Bells on the Hill
Cowboy's Bride
One Stubborn Cowboy
Crazy About a Cowboy
Never Doubt a Cowboy
Cowboy Marshal
Summer Cowboy
Second Chance Cowboy
Movie Star Cowboy

Tropical Escape Series
Island Rendezvous
Come into the Sun
Island Paradise
Destination Romance Boxed Set

Rocky Point Series
The Family Next Door
Rocky Point Reunion
Rocky Point Promise
Rocky Point Hero

Elite Security Mystery Series
Trusting Jake

The Ultimate Billionaires
The Cynical Sheikh
Falling for the Sheikh
A Sheikh of Her Own
The Unforgettable Sheikh

Other Books
A Soldier's Christmas
I'll Take Forever
Jared's Promise
The Paper Marriage
The Christmas Locket
The Banished Bride
Cowboy Charade
The Cowboy's Special Christmas
Mail Order Bride
Because of You

Printed in Great Britain
by Amazon